W9-BVX-300

TIA AND TAMERA MOWRY

TWINTUITION
DOUBLE DARE

HARPER
An Imprint of HarperCollinsPublishers

Twintuition: Double Dare
Copyright © 2017 by Dashon Productions and Two Heart Productions
All rights reserved. Printed in the United States of America.
No part of this book may be used or reproduced in any manner whatsoever
without written permission except in the case of brief quotations embodied in
critical articles and reviews. For information address HarperCollins Children's
Books, a division of HarperCollins Publishers, 195 Broadway, New York, NY
10007.
www.harpercollinschildrens.com

Library of Congress Control Number: 2016957944

ISBN 978-0-06-237293-2

Typography by Carla Weise
18 19 20 21 22   CG/BRR   10 9 8 7 6 5 4 3 2 1
❖
First paperback edition, 2018

CHILDREN'S ROOM

I dedicate this book to my incredible son, Cree, and my lovely and supportive husband, Cory.

—Tia

To my entire family—my mother, Darlene; father, Timothy; my brothers, Tahj and Tavior; sister, Tia; husband, Adam; son, Aden; and daughter, Ariah.

—Tamera

3 9222 03157 5546

1

CASSIE

THE ONE WORD my friends would never use to describe me is *speechless*. But as I stared at the older woman standing in the middle of my tiny front yard, I might as well have been mute.

"Cassandra, I presume?" said the woman who had just introduced herself as our Grandmother Lockwood.

"Wow, do you have it, too?" my identical twin sister, Caitlyn, blurted out. She and our mother were standing right behind me on the stoop. "You know—like, extrasensory powers?"

Mom looked surprised. But I was too distracted to worry about that.

"So, I see my guess was correct." Our grandmother smiled a tight-lipped little smile at me, then turned to my sister. "Then I suppose you're Caitlyn. It's wonderful to see you both again after so many years."

I wished I could say the same, but I didn't remember her at all.

"What are you doing here, Verity?" Mom pushed past us, facing off against the older woman. "I thought I told you—"

"And I told *you*, Deidre," Grandmother Lockwood said icily, lifting her chin and looking down her long, narrow nose at Mom, "it's important that the girls know their heritage. We've already waited too long in my opinion." She raised one thin, pale eyebrow. "An opinion that is rather more educated about these matters than yours, I might add."

"You—I—but—" Mom sputtered.

Caitlyn and I glanced at each other. Our faces

always look almost the same—identical twins, right?—but at the moment her stunned expression was a mirror image of my own. On top of everything else, this woman had *interrupted* our mother? And was still standing? Even more shocking, Mom currently appeared fairly speechless herself, which happens to her even less often than it does to me. She never would have made it through twenty years in the military otherwise—not to mention the police academy.

"Now, girls." Grandmother Lockwood stepped toward us. "We have much to talk about."

"Wait," I blurted out, suddenly realizing something. "Lockwood . . ." I looked at Cait again. "That's the family from, like, England or somewhere that you keep talking about, right? Are we talking about the same Lockwoods?"

It hardly seemed possible. Cait had found out about the Lockwoods online. They were a family with special powers. *Very* special.

"I saw something about the Lockwoods on a message board," Caitlyn told our grandmother, sounding rather shy. Again, not normal.

"Yes, I'm aware of that." Grandmother Lockwood pursed her lips. "Fortunately my nephew—your father's cousin—spotted it immediately and was able to take care of it."

My mind was still trying to catch up with all this. What was happening here? Was this snooty British woman really our father's mom? The whole idea was just too weird. Especially since, up until recently, I hadn't even known we had a grandmother other than Maw Maw Jean.

I mean, I guess we had to have another one, but our dad had died when Caitlyn and I were babies. I suppose we'd always assumed his parents were long gone, too.

Only it turned out that we assumed wrong. A little over a week ago, totally out of the blue, a package had arrived addressed to the two of us. Inside were three things—a key-shaped necklace, an old leather-bound book, and a letter from a grandmother we never knew about, the same woman who was now standing in our yard.

And now, we'd just come home from our birthday party at my friend Megan's pool when suddenly a taxi had pulled up in front of our house and Grandmother Lockwood stepped out.

That was weird enough, since we'd recently moved from San Antonio to tiny Aura, Texas, which was miles from civilization, including taxi dispatchers. The weirder part? I'd already seen her arrival happen. At least sort of.

I forgot about that when Mom stomped forward. "Verity, enough."

She seemed to have recovered her voice. And her attitude. "I told you, things are under control here. You ought to go home and let me handle *my* children." She glared at the old woman.

Grandmother Lockwood barely glanced at her. "The closest hotel I could find is in a town called Six Oaks," she told Cait and me. "Do you know where that is?"

I nodded. Aura is so small that it doesn't have its own mall, hospital, or basically anything else you'd want to find. Including, apparently, a hotel.

"Yeah, it's a few miles from here," I told her.

"Good." Grandmother Lockwood took a few steps toward her taxi, which had been idling at the curb this whole time. "I'm off to check in and recover from my flight. But I'll call for you tomorrow. Are you free for brunch, perhaps?"

"Okay," Caitlyn said eagerly. "Are you sure you can't stay right now? We have so many questions—"

"Hold on!" Mom blurted out. "Listen, Verity—"

"What on Earth is the problem, Deidre?" the older woman responded coolly. "Am I not allowed to take my granddaughters to brunch to celebrate their birthday?"

Mom sputtered some more at that. Cait was watching her, looking worried. Uh-oh. My sister and I may look almost identical, but our personalities are anything but. For instance, my sister is nothing if not a peacemaker. The last thing I wanted was for Caitlyn to say something stupid, like that we didn't want to go to brunch after all, in order to make that blustery look on Mom's face go away.

"We'll be there," I told Grandmother Lockwood

quickly, stepping down off the stoop to face her. She was only a couple of inches taller than me, even though I'd just turned twelve that day. "I mean, thank you. We'd love to have brunch with you."

"Wonderful." She reached out and patted my arm. Her skin was papery-dry and cool, but I barely felt it.

That was because it was happening again.

Buzzing filled my head, drowning out everything else. Even though she was right in front of me, Grandmother Lockwood's face faded out to a dim blur. In its place, I saw a much sharper version of her standing in a fancy-looking room. She was on the phone, looking disgruntled as she listened to whatever the person on the other end of the line was saying.

As she pulled her hand away, I staggered back, gulping for air. Visions always left me a little confused and freaked out. At least it wasn't as bad now, though. When the visions first started happening, I'd thought I was losing my mind. Not that the truth was much less crazy . . .

Grandmother Lockwood gave me a sharp look but didn't say anything. Why not? Did she realize I'd just had a vision? After all, she was the first person who'd seemed to know anything about the weird ability Caitlyn and I had both developed lately. Namely, the ability to see the future—whether we wanted to or not.

"I'll be back for you tomorrow at ten a.m. sharp." Grandmother Lockwood eyed my mother as if daring her to protest.

Mom glared back at her. "Fine," she spat out. "Brunch. But I'm coming too, and that's that." She narrowed her eyes, as if expecting Grandmother Lockwood to protest.

The old woman waved one thin hand. "Of course," she said. "I absolutely insist you join us, Deidre."

Mom blinked. "And we need to have a little talk first. Just you and me." Uh-oh. Yeah, Mom seemed to be recovering, all right. She was using what Cait and I call her scarymama voice now. It's enough to stop me in my tracks and bring my sister to tears. Or vice versa.

Grandmother Lockwood? Immune, apparently.

"Fine, fine, but it will have to wait until the morning. I'm exhausted." The old woman started to turn away. Then she stopped. "One more thing, girls. I sent you a package, but it was returned." She shot Mom another raised eyebrow. "Did you see it?"

"Yes," Caitlyn said eagerly. "We got it. But . . ." She trailed off, giving Mom a vaguely guilty look.

"I see. Then by chance do you still have the Lockwood family talisman? It wasn't in the package when it came back."

Mom looked startled. "Family talisman?" she echoed. "What's that?"

Grandmother Lockwood ignored her. Again, not something most people would dare to do. But I was quickly figuring out that Grandmother Lockwood wasn't most people.

Caitlyn was already stepping forward, her hand reaching for the thin silver chain around her neck. "Yes, we have it," she said, pulling out the pendant from beneath her shirt.

I shivered when I saw it. Lockwood family talisman, huh? So we were right. Cait and I had already figured out that our visions got stronger when we were wearing that thing. A lot stronger.

"Where did you get that?" Mom sounded a little hysterical now. "What is it? Verity, I demand that you—"

"Tomorrow," Grandmother Lockwood cut her off firmly. "We'll discuss it all—tomorrow." She nodded at Cait, who was still holding the talisman. "Keep that safe. It's irreplaceable."

"Um, okay?" Caitlyn said. But Grandmother Lockwood was already striding back toward her cab.

I sank down onto the front step, my mind whirling. "Wow," I said. "I can't believe she's here."

Mom glowered at us, opening her mouth as if to say something. Or to start yelling, more likely. Fine. I was ready to do a little yelling myself. Now that our grandmother was here, it was more than obvious that Mom had known about this crazy vision thing. And she'd never told us about it. Never warned us. How could she do that? Mom and I had a tendency to butt heads at times, especially when she got all strict about stupid stuff like curfews and makeup. But even when I didn't agree with her decisions, I'd always trusted that she was trying to do what she thought was right. But how could she possibly think it was right to keep us in the dark about something so important?

I was more than ready to have it out with her if she wanted—scarymama or not. But Mom snapped her mouth shut again without saying a word. Spinning on her heel, she stormed back into the house and slammed the door behind her. Cait's eyes were wide.

"Whoa," she said. "She seems mad. Like, for real."

"Gee, ya think?" I rolled my eyes. "Obviously she didn't want us to even know our grandmother exists. No duh that she's a little peeved when the woman herself just shows up on our doorstep and starts talking about talismans and stuff."

Cait stepped closer. "By the way, did you have a vision just now?"

I grimaced. "Yeah. Just Granny Lockwood on the phone, no biggie."

That was how the visions worked. They happened seemingly randomly—we would touch someone, and bam, there it was. We would see a scene from that person's future. How far in the future was anybody's guess. And what we saw ranged from super-important stuff, like Mom almost losing her job or a friend being hurt, to stupid trivia like someone getting a bad grade on a test or whatever. We couldn't control the visions, like, at all.

At least, we hadn't been able to control them so far. That letter from our grandmother had mentioned teaching us to get a handle on our abilities. Or something like that—Mom had grabbed it away before we'd read more than the first few lines. Speaking of which . . .

"You know, we might want to keep an eye on Mom," I told Caitlyn. "I wouldn't put it past her to pack us up and move to Timbuktu tonight to avoid that brunch. Or maybe put out a hit on Granny L. Just saying." I was only half joking. It wasn't easy to wrap my head around the fact that Mom had hidden a whole entire grandmother from us all this time. I wouldn't be getting over that anytime soon.

Caitlyn bit her lip. "Don't make Mom mad, okay, Cass?" she pleaded. "I mean, this has to be a shock for her, too."

Instead of promising anything of the sort, I got up and hurried inside without responding. Caitlyn followed.

Mom was pacing around the tiny living room with her cell phone pressed to her ear, apparently mid-rant. "—and I was afraid this might happen. That woman never could take no for an answer, even though I'm just trying to protect them from what happened to—"

As soon as she saw us, she frowned—well, more than she already was, anyway—and stopped talking. Then she headed for the back hall.

"Hang on, Cheryl," she snapped. "The walls have ears."

Cheryl was her sister, our aunt, who still lived in our old neighborhood in San Antonio. So she was in on this, too?

Mom disappeared into the bathroom, clicking

the lock and then turning on the shower full blast. I pressed my ear to the door, but all I could hear was mumbling.

Caitlyn watched me. "So much for Mom's good mood," she said softly.

"Yeah, seriously," I muttered, flopping onto the sofa.

Our birthday had gone really well up until the moment Grandmother Lockwood climbed out of that cab. We'd had a big pool party for all our friends, and had even managed to stop something bad from happening to one of those friends, thanks to our visions.

Caitlyn and I had already figured out one thing. Seeing the future meant being able to *change* the future. At least if we could puzzle out what we were actually seeing, which wasn't always easy.

"Do you think our grandmother . . ." I paused for a second. Saying that still felt weird. "Do you think she'll be able to tell us more about our visions?"

Cait brightened. "I hope so! That's what she had said in the letter she sent us."

"You mean the letter she tried to send us." I clenched my fists, thinking back to the way Mom had snatched Grandmother Lockwood's package out of our hands, even though it had been addressed to us. Totally not fair. But then again, Mom had done a lot of not-fair stuff over the years, as we'd just discovered . . .

At that moment Mom emerged from the bathroom, her expression still stormy. Hopping to my feet, I stomped toward her, my own expression matching hers, as I got fired up all over again.

"Well?" I demanded. "Are you going to stick to your word and let us go tomorrow or what?"

"Cass!" Caitlyn whispered, sounding horrified.

I knew why. Mom hated when we sassed her. But this was way beyond sass. "Because we can't keep going like this," I blurted out before I even knew what I was going to say. "Seriously, Mom, you can't keep secrets like this, okay? Because we're having all these wackadoodle visions lately, Cait and me both. And they're getting worse . . ."

The words poured out of me as I babbled on

about the visions for a while. How they'd started about six months earlier. How Caitlyn and I had figured out we were both having them. How they were getting more frequent—and more vivid.

Behind Mom, Caitlyn looked alarmed and a little queasy. We hadn't told Mom any of this before today, and I guess me suddenly spilling my guts took Cait by surprise.

But Mom didn't look surprised at all. She just listened.

". . . so anyway," I finished, clenching my fists at my sides. "We have to know what's happening. We have to talk to our grandmother."

I braced myself for her response, determined to hold my ground, no matter what. What was the worst Mom could do? Ground me forever?

But she just sighed, her shoulders slumped, and she looked almost . . . defeated.

"I was afraid something like this might happen," she said with a shrug. "In any case, your grandmother came all this way to see you. I won't stand in the way if y'all want to get to know each other. Maybe there's no point in trying to protect you anymore."

I traded a shocked glance with Caitlyn.

"Protect us from what?" I asked, but Mom stayed silent.

"So—so we can go to brunch?" Cait added cautiously.

Mom shrugged again. "Of course. If you want to go, I'm not going to stop you."

I opened my mouth to repeat my question. But then I closed it again, deciding not to push it.

For now.

2
CAITLYN

MY HEAD WAS still spinning as I crawled into bed that night. Cassie was perched at her desk across the room fiddling with her cell phone. Our house in Aura only has two bedrooms, which meant Cass and I were sharing a room again for the first time since we were six years old. At first we'd both been less than thrilled about that. For one thing, Cassie seems to have inherited Mom's military obsession with keeping things neat and tidy. While I, um, didn't. I definitely hadn't been looking forward to coming home and finding my socks alphabetized and my school notebooks spit-shined.

But that wasn't the only reason. When Cassie and I were little, we hadn't just shared a room. We'd shared everything—every thought, every feeling, every minute of the day, pretty much. It had been us against the world, best friends as well as sisters.

When had that changed? I wasn't sure. Sometime along the way I guess we just grew apart. By the time we'd moved to San Antonio a few years ago, we were living almost totally separate lives. So sharing a bedroom again? *Awk* with a capital *Ward*.

But now I was actually glad we were stuck in this room together. It gave us a chance to get to know each other again. Besides that, it gave us time to talk about what was happening. And lately, a lot of stuff was happening.

"So . . . ," I said. "We have a grandmother. Another one, I mean."

Cassie glanced at me. "Yeah. Weird, right?"

"Totally." I sat up and hugged my knees. "Maybe now we'll finally get some answers about what's happening to us. Maybe Grandmother Lockwood can teach us to control our visions!"

Cassie wrinkled her nose. "Grandmother Lock-wood?" she said. "Do we really have to call her that?"

"What else are we supposed to call her? That's her name."

"Yeah, and Maw Maw Jean's real name is Mrs. Jeanetta Robinson Waters. Doesn't mean she wants us to call her that."

"True. But I can't quite picture calling our new grandma, like, Mee Maw VeeVee or something, you know?"

Cassie grinned. "I'd love to see her face if we did, though."

"No!" Half laughing and half horrified, I jumped up and hurried over to poke her in the arm. "Promise me you won't. Seriously, Cass, if we make her mad she might decide to—"

"Relax." She cut me off with a snort. "I'm not that clueless, okay?"

"Fine." I slouched against the edge of her desk. "I just don't want to mess this up, you know?" My hand wandered up to touch the talisman I was still wearing around my neck, tracing the intricate carving of a star on the top part. "I mean, maybe we'll finally get to learn something about our dad!"

"I know, right?" Cass reached over and squeezed my hand.

Suddenly, everything was drowned out by loud buzzing in my head. The Cassie sitting in front of me shorted out, fading away behind a super-vivid image of a different Cassie. This one was in the school cafeteria. She was dancing wildly, waving her arms around. A bunch of her friends were standing around, staring at her intently.

I guess she noticed what was happening. She yanked her hand away, and the vision was gone.

"What?" she demanded. "Did you just have one?"

I nodded, unable to speak for a second. My hand was still clutching the talisman.

"Well?" Cassie looked impatient.

I swallowed hard. "It—it was about you."

"Duh." She rolled her eyes. Probably because that was how the visions worked—they were always about the person we were touching. "Was it something good?"

She frowned slightly. Cassie has a chip on her shoulder about how our visions usually play out. It hadn't taken us long to realize that Cassie mostly seems to see bad things happening to people, while I mostly see good stuff. Ever since, she acts like that's my fault. Then again, she's always had an attitude about the way I try to make the best of things. Probably because she's more of a glass-half-empty girl herself.

"I don't really know if it was good or not," I said slowly. Then I described what I'd seen.

By the time I finished, Cassie looked as if she couldn't decide whether to laugh or scowl. "Okay," she said. "Did I have rhythm, at least?"

"I don't know," I said. "I mean, you know how it works, with the buzzing, so if there was music I . . ."

"Chill, I'm just kidding." She shook her head. "Anyway, I guess it's a good thing we'll be getting some answers tomorrow. If your vision is telling us I'm going to totally embarrass myself at school soon, maybe Queen Verity can help me figure out how to stop it from happening."

"You're not going to call her that either, are you?" I asked before I could stop myself.

She didn't bother to respond. Instead she just said, "I'm bushed," and headed toward her bed. "Better get some sleep before the big brunch."

"IS SHE HERE yet?" Cassie peered out the front window by the couch the next morning.

"It's only nine fifty-five," I pointed out. "I'm sure she'll be here soon."

My phone vibrated in my pocket. I pulled it out and saw that it was my friend Liam calling.

Liam O'Day had been one of the first people I'd met in Aura. We'd hit it off quickly, and I considered him one of my best friends. Cassie? Well, she considered him a classic nerd. Just another example of how different we were these days. She loved being part of the popular crowd, while I didn't care about that at all.

Even so, I almost hit ignore, since I knew

Grandmother Lockwood would be there any minute. And I wasn't sure I was up to telling him about her just yet. She was too wrapped up with the visions, and I definitely hadn't told him about any of that. At first, when I'd thought it was just me seeing things, I hadn't wanted my new friends to think I was crazy. Once I'd discovered that Cassie was having the visions, too, it hadn't seemed right to share our secret without her permission. And since she hadn't breathed a word about it to her friends, I knew she wouldn't want me sharing with mine.

My finger hovered over the ignore button, then hit the one to answer instead. Cassie was still staring outside looking impatient, so I figured I had time. "Hi, Liam," I said.

"Hi, Caitlyn," Liam's cheerful voice greeted me. "I'm just calling to say thanks for inviting me to the party yesterday. I had a great time."

"Oh! You're welcome." Leave it to Liam to be Mr. Polite. "Thanks for coming and thanks for the books, too. They look really good; I already started one of them."

That was a little white lie. Yesterday after the party, things had gotten intense fast, what with Grandmother Lockwood's unexpected arrival. I'd almost forgotten about the birthday gifts Liam and my other friends had given me. But I figured he didn't need to know that.

"Cool, I hope you like them," he said. "So what's on the agenda for your first full day as an official twelve-year-old?"

"Oh, this and that," I said. Just then Cassie spun around from her position at the window, gesturing excitedly. "Um, actually Mom is taking Cass and me to brunch over in Six Oaks." At least part of that wasn't a lie, I told myself. I already felt bad that I wasn't able to tell him about the visions. He was exactly the kind of person who would have found something like that super interesting—and the type who'd never judge us for it, either.

"That sounds fun," Liam said. "When are you going?"

"Right now, actually. Sorry, I'd better hang up—Cassie gets cranky if you make her wait for her bacon." Ignoring the face my sister was making at me, I added, "I'll see you at school tomorrow."

As I stuck the phone back in my pocket, Mom came charging out of the kitchen. "Is she here?" she demanded. Not waiting for a response, she pointed at me and Cass. "Stay," she ordered in her best Officer Waters voice. "I need to talk to your grandmother alone for a moment before we go."

"Okay," I said. Not that it mattered. Mom was already on her way outside.

Cassie took a couple of steps toward the door. "No way," she said. "We can't let her talk Granny L into leaving or something."

I grabbed her arm. "Stop," I said. "Just let them talk. I'm sure it'll be fine."

She gave me the stink eye. "Thanks, Susie Sunshine," she said. "Somehow I'm not so sure. Mom can be very persuasive, you know. And she obviously doesn't want our grandmother here."

"So?" I shrugged. "Grandmother Lockwood doesn't exactly seem like a pushover. Mom tried to get her to leave yesterday, and you saw how well that worked."

"Hmm." Cassie still sounded dubious as she returned to her spot at the window. "Whoa, check it out—she must've rented a limo."

I joined her, peering out at the big, shiny black car at the curb. "I'm not surprised," I said with a smile. "She doesn't really seem like the yellow cab type."

We watched as Mom and Grandmother Lockwood talked by the car. In Mom's case, that involved plenty of gesturing, though our grandmother mostly just stood there with her arms crossed.

"This is making me nervous," Cass said after a few minutes. "I'm going out there."

"Cassie, no!" I exclaimed. "Look, I think they're finished anyway. See?"

Mom was striding back toward the house. Grandmother Lockwood stayed where she was, watching her go. I held my breath. Was Cassie right? Had Mom actually talked our grandmother into changing plans?

A second later the front door swung open. "Time to go, girls," Mom called briskly.

"You mean you didn't scare her off?" Cassie muttered.

I winced. Luckily Mom had already turned to head back toward the limo, so she didn't hear her.

"Cool it, okay?" I told Cassie as I grabbed a sweater. "If you get all rude and pushy, Mom might pull the plug on this whole deal for real. Just try to chill."

"No promises." She hurried outside.

With a sigh, I followed. The limo driver had climbed out to open the passenger-side door for Grandmother Lockwood. When he saw us coming, he smiled and bowed.

"Ladies, right this way," he called, stepping over to open the back door. He was a stout man in his fifties with a big, crooked nose and a pronounced Texas drawl. "My name is Al, and I have the honor of being your chauffeur today."

"Hi, Al, nice to meet you," I said with a smile. Cassie just muttered a quick "hi" and hopped into the backseat after Mom and Grandmother Lockwood.

When I followed them in, I looked around with interest. I'd never ridden in a limo before.

"Nice car," Cassie told our grandmother, who was buckling herself in beside Mom in the seat across from us.

"Yes, well, I'll need a way to get around while I'm in the States," she replied. "And I'm certainly not going to try driving on the wrong side of the road at my age." Glancing over her shoulder at Al, she added, "The hotel, please, Mr. Simpson."

"Sure thing, Miz Lockwood." Al started the car. "Beautiful day for a drive, isn't it, ladies?"

"Yes, lovely." Mom sounded tense as she answered.

I glanced at Cassie. She looked tense, too. Her hands were clutched in her lap, and she was staring at our grandmother. I guessed she was dying to start bombarding her with questions. I just hoped she could control herself, or Driver Al was going to get an earful.

Good thing Six Oaks is only, like, twenty minutes away, I thought, leaning back and doing my best to enjoy the ride.

3

CASSIE

THE SIX OAKS Plaza was surprisingly swanky for
small-town Central Texas. At least six stories tall,
with a gold-pillared entrance and huge potted palms
on either side of the door, it wouldn't have seemed
out of place in Dallas or LA.

"Nice place," I murmured, glad I'd decided to
wear a skirt.

We climbed out of the limo and a uniformed
doorman ushered us inside. Grandmother Lockwood thanked him with a nod, then gestured for us

to follow her across the hushed, carpeted lobby.

The hotel restaurant was just as fancy as the rest of the place. Soft music was playing, and the servers all wore three-piece suits. Yeah, even the women.

Soon we were seated in a plush booth in the corner. I couldn't help noticing that we were separated from the other diners by an empty table. Had Grandmother Lockwood arranged that so we'd be able to talk without anyone hearing? Good, because we had a lot to talk about.

Not wanting to waste any time with stupid questions about school or other small talk, I decided to dive right in. "So, Grandmother," I said as soon as the server had taken our orders. "Can you see the future, too? Or just us?"

"Cassie!" Caitlyn widened her eyes at me, and Mom frowned but didn't say anything.

Grandmother Lockwood took a sip of her water, unfazed by my questions. "No, I married into the Lockwood family. It was my brother-in-law who had the Sight in my generation."

"Okay," I said. "So then did—"

"Wait," she cut me off sternly. "There's a lot to cover. Perhaps I'd better give you the important information, and then if there's time, you may ask questions."

I don't like being told to sit down and shut up and I almost told her so. Almost. But I decided maybe she was right. Caitlyn and I had been feeling our way along so far, but we still barely knew what was going on. Maybe we didn't even know what questions to ask.

Anyway, my grandmother was already talking again. "Nobody knows how long the Sight has run in the Lockwood family," she said. "At least a dozen generations, probably more."

"Wow," Caitlyn murmured.

"Nobody knows where it came from, or exactly how it works," she continued. "In the past, people didn't talk about such things in public."

"As opposed to now, when we blab about it to anyone who'll listen," I said sarcastically.

"Cassandra," Mom said warningly.

Just then the server reappeared carrying a huge

tray loaded with food. For a moment, we were all busy sorting out our orders.

"As I was saying," Grandmother Lockwood continued once the server disappeared again, "at certain times in history, speaking of the Sight might have resulted in hanging or decapitation, most likely preceded by torture and shaming."

Mom cleared her throat. "Verity, is it really necessary to—"

"The girls must know what the dangers are," Grandmother Lockwood cut her off sharply. "And why it's so important to keep the family secrets."

Again, interrupting Mom? Speaking of danger . . .

Mom glowered, and for a second I thought she was about to let the old woman have it. Instead, she sighed and started picking at her omelet.

Grandmother Lockwood continued as if the interruption had never happened. The lady was cool as a cucumber in January, that was for sure.

"As best we know, the Sight is passed down in the blood or genes," she said. "But only one person per generation inherits it." She paused to look down her nose at Cait and me. "Until now, anyway."

"So how did you know we were the ones?" Caitlyn asked, leaning forward so far that her hair almost touched her waffles. "I mean, if your husband's brother had it, wouldn't it be more likely to pass down to one of his kids—and grandkids?"

I waited for Grandmother Lockwood to tell her to be quiet. But the old woman just shook her head. "It doesn't always work that way." Grandmother Lockwood fiddled with the stem of her water goblet, then shot Mom a quick glance.

"Your father had the Sight," Mom put in grimly.

I gasped. "What? And you're just telling us this *now*?"

Mom shrugged. "It wasn't my idea to tell you at all."

No kidding. I glared at her briefly, but Grandmother Lockwood was talking again.

"Yes, your father had the gift," she said softly, a faraway look in her gray eyes. "For all the good it did him."

What was that supposed to mean? I was kind of

afraid to ask. Was that why our father had died so young? Had the Sight caused it somehow? Or at least failed to warn him so he could stop it? I shivered, and it wasn't from the air-conditioning.

Caitlyn was chewing her lower lip in that way she does when she's thinking hard. "Wow," she said. "So our dad had it. And his uncle had it."

"That's correct." Grandmother Lockwood nodded. "It's not always passed down directly. So there's always a bit of a guessing game when the new generation comes along. You two have several cousins in the UK, and—"

"Several?" I blurted out, a little overwhelmed by all this new info. "How many is several?"

"We can get into that later if there's time." She sipped her water. "The point is, the youngest of those cousins is several years older than you two."

Again with the several! But Caitlyn was nodding.

"So our cousins all turned twelve already," she said, putting the pieces together. "And they don't have the Sight."

"Correct. That's how we knew it had to be you." She glanced from Cait to me and back again. "Of course, we initially assumed it would be only one of you."

"Okay, back to our dad for a sec," I said. "Did the Sight have something to do with why he died? I mean, you said it could be dangerous, and . . ."

"All in due time," Grandmother Lockwood said.

"Due time?" I dropped my fork, fed up with her non-answers. "Come on! You came all this way— enough with the secrets!"

Grandmother Lockwood traded a look with Mom. "I understand that you want to know more about John."

At our blank looks, Mom added, "Your father. John Thompson Lockwood."

John Thompson Lockwood. Caitlyn looked stunned, as if she hadn't realized he'd had a name other than Dad. I knew how she felt. We'd always thought his name was John Thompson, which I guess it was, sort of. But somehow, I'd never thought about him that way. Just as "Dad" or "our father" or whatever.

Once again, Grandmother Lockwood's expression softened slightly. "I can tell you this—he was a wonderful person."

"True that," Mom put in quietly, stabbing at her omelet.

"Tell us more," Caitlyn begged. "Please. What was he like?"

"John was a delightful child, friendly and intelligent. I'd hoped the family gift might bypass him, but he had his first vision a few months before he turned twelve." Grandmother Lockwood smiled wistfully. "He handed me a flower he'd picked for me, and saw me getting a surprise visit from an old friend."

"So he only saw good things?" Caitlyn asked.

Our grandmother blinked. "What?"

"Good things," Cait said again. "Like me."

Mom and Grandmother Lockwood looked mystified. "What are you talking about?" Mom asked.

I realized I hadn't really gotten into that part when I'd told her about our visions the day before. "Yeah, it's awesome," I said with a snort. "Cait gets to see all the happy happy joy joy stuff that's going to happen to people, and I only get the doom and gloom."

Grandmother Lockwood leaned forward, her eyes sharp. "Is this true?"

"Sort of," Cait admitted, shooting me a worried look. "I mean, we think so. We're pretty sure."

"Fascinating!" The old woman sat back, staring up at the ceiling for a moment.

I tapped my fingers on the table. "But anyway, you were talking about our dad and the visions . . . ," I prompted.

"Oh, yes." She blinked and sat up. "After that first vision, the Sight visited him sporadically for a while. Of course, by then his uncle had already taken him under his wing, prepared him for what was to come . . ." She paused to glare briefly at Mom. "So he was ready when the visions became more frequent and intense."

That didn't sound good. "Frequent?" I said.

"Intense?" Caitlyn blurted out at the same time.

"Yes. Typically, the twelfth birthday and the months thereafter can be a bit—er—chaotic."

Great. Just great. So the visions might get even worse?

I was about to ask, but Grandmother Lockwood

had more memories of Dad to share, and I didn't want to interrupt. She told us how he'd used the visions to help prevent a house fire, then switched gears to some stories about his school friends and stuff. Some of them involved visions, but most of them didn't—they were just regular stories about a kid who sounded pretty cool. Our dad.

Mom kept quiet through all this, her eyes mostly on her food, but I was pretty sure I saw her smile a few times. Caitlyn had forgotten about her food entirely; she'd dropped her fork on her plate and was leaning forward, eating up every word our grandmother said.

I was pretty spellbound by the stories myself. I wanted to change the subject back to the Sight, but I also didn't. We hadn't known much of anything about our dad until now, including his rather large Lockwood family.

That reminded me . . . "Why aren't we Lockwoods?" I blurted out when Grandmother Lockwood paused to take a bite of her food. "I mean, our last name."

She glanced at Mom. "You were at first," she said.

"But after what happened to John, well, your mother got nervous."

Mom finally looked up from her brunch. "Can you blame me?" Her tone was challenging.

"What happened to him?" I asked.

"You might not have grown up with the Lockwood name," Grandmother Lockwood went on without answering my question. "But you're Lockwoods, and that means we have work to do. You need to get control of your powers."

"Great!" Cait exclaimed. "We've been hoping—"

"Wait." Mom pointed her fork at our grandmother. "I thought we were going to hold off on that, Verity."

"I said we'd discuss it." Grandmother Lockwood dabbed her mouth with her napkin. "That's what I'm doing now."

Mom gritted her teeth. "Not with the girls, we're not."

"Sorry, Deidre, but there's no time to waste." Grandmother Lockwood glanced at her watch. "Speaking of which, I'm afraid I must go."

"What?" I exclaimed. "But we have so many questions! You've hardly told us anything!"

"All in due time." I was getting pretty tired of that phrase already. "Right now, I have business to attend to. I'll contact you tomorrow."

"Tomorrow is Monday." Mom sounded kind of aggressive. "They have school. And I'm working tomorrow night and have to leave at four. Whatever you want to talk to them about, I need to be there."

Grandmother Lockwood was already gesturing for the server to bring the check. "Tomorrow," she said again. "I'll be in touch after school." With a glance at Mom, she added, "And before four o'clock."

4
CAITLYN

IT'S NOT EVERY day you find out you have a whole family you didn't know existed. By the time Cassie and I got to school the next morning, I still couldn't quite wrap my mind around it.

"Do you think she'll come over this afternoon?" I asked as we entered. "Grandmother Lockwood, I mean."

"She said so, right?" Cassie elbowed me. "Chill. We'll talk about this later."

Several of our fellow sixth graders were barreling

toward us. "Twins!" cried a girl I barely knew from Cassie's homeroom. "Your party was awesome!"

Right behind her were Cassie's friends Megan March and Lavender Adams. "Yeah, everyone's still talking about it." Lavender sounded smug, probably because the party had been her idea. Then again, she always kind of sounds that way.

"Thanks again for hosting it," Cass told Megan.

"Yeah, ditto," I added. Lavender wasn't my favorite person in town, but Megan actually seemed pretty nice. Her mom was the mayor of Aura, and her uncle was the chief of police. In other words, Aura royalty.

Lavender linked her arm through Cassie's. "I took a bunch of pictures at the party and uploaded them," she said. "We should decide which ones turned out the best."

I tuned out as the three of them started chattering about angles and fashion and stuff. Meanwhile more kids were crowding around wanting to talk about the party. And behind the others, I noticed Gabe Campbell skulking around.

He met my eye with a smirk, and I shivered. Last week, Cassie and I had ducked into an empty classroom to talk about our visions. When we came out, Gabe was lurking just outside. We still weren't sure whether he'd heard anything.

I really hoped not. Because Gabe was about the last person I wanted to know our secret. See, the reason we moved to Aura in the first place was because Mom got offered a job on the town police force. The reason? Gabe's uncle had just been fired for embezzling. And somehow Gabe blamed Mom, and hated us by association.

Okay, I know that doesn't make much sense. But Gabe's the kind of guy who always seems to be looking for any excuse to get offended and cranky.

Right now he didn't look that cranky, though. In fact, he looked pleased with himself. I wasn't sure what that was about, and it worried me a little. But there wasn't much I could do about it.

Just then I heard shouts. Four guys were bounding toward us—Brayden Diaz and his friends Biff, Buzz, and Brent. They were on the football team together, and everyone called them the B Boys. Actually, only three of them were bounding. Brayden had broken his leg in a football game recently, so he was hobbling behind them.

"Hey, guys," Lavender called to them. "Great party the other day, huh?"

"What?" Biff blinked at her, then glanced at Cassie and me. "Oh yeah, right. Awesome."

"But listen, big news," Brent put in. "Did you guys hear about the Truth or Dare thing?"

"What Truth or Dare thing?" Megan asked.

"It's this huge craze over at the high school," Brayden said. "It started with just a few people, but now everyone's daring each other to do all kinds of crazy stuff!"

Biff nodded. "My brother told me about it." He grinned, flicking back his dark hair. "He wasn't going to let me play, but then he dared me to do his chores last night. Total drag, but at least it got me in the game, right? That means it's my turn to pick someone."

Lavender wrinkled her nose. "I don't get it."

"Truth or Dare," Buzz told her. "You know, you pick someone, say 'truth or dare,' and—"

"I know what Truth or Dare is, you dolt," Lavender snapped. "But why is everyone at the high school playing?"

"Nobody can turn down a cool dare, I guess." Biff shrugged, then tapped his finger on his chin. "Now, who should I pick?"

Before he could decide, Principal Zale came into the lobby. He spotted us gathered there and strode over.

"Homerooms, people," he said briskly. "The bell's about to ring."

"Okay, okay," Biff said. "Guess I'll have to pick someone at lunch." With a wink, he turned away.

The entire sixth grade is divided into two sections, which means only two homerooms. So the group pretty much split into two big blobs and headed in opposite directions.

I waved good-bye to Cassie, who was in the other section with Megan and Brayden. Then I followed Lavender and the other B Boys toward our homeroom. Gabe was in my section, too, but he'd disappeared.

Halfway down the hall, I spotted Liam and our friend Bianca Ramos at Bianca's locker. "Hi, Cassie," Liam said in his usual cheerful way. "We were just talking about the class trip."

Bianca nodded, closing her locker door. "I can't believe it's coming up so soon."

"Right." I'd almost forgotten about it; my head was still too full of everything I'd learned yesterday. I wished I knew for sure that Grandmother Lockwood was coming over later. She'd said something about having to take care of some business. What if she couldn't make it after all?

Liam grinned. "It must be weird for you," he said.

I was startled, thinking for a second that he was talking about the whole surprise-grandmother-visit thing. "Wh-what?" I stammered.

"Going to San Antonio?" Liam waggled his reddish eyebrows. "I mean, that's your old hometown, right?"

"Oh. Right." Next Thursday, the entire grade

was going to San Antonio for the day. It would be kind of weird being there again, now that he mentioned it. But I couldn't seem to focus on that.

"Anyway, I heard we'll be going to the Alamo, and then . . . ," Liam began.

I kind of stopped listening, my mind wandering back to yesterday. Grandmother Lockwood hadn't really told us much, but it was more than we'd known before. Cassie and I hadn't been able to stop talking about it after brunch. I just wished Mom hadn't rushed off to the precinct the second we got home. Had she really just remembered she had to take care of some paperwork, or was she trying to avoid our questions? Either way, she hadn't returned until dinnertime, and by then Cassie and I had agreed not to discuss it in front of her. Actually, Cassie was the one who'd decided that, and I'd agreed to go along with it to keep the peace. If only for the moment anyway.

At least we know our dad's real name now, I thought, *and that he had the same kind of visions we're having.*

I shivered, feeling closer to him than ever before.

I hoped today Grandmother Lockwood would tell us more stories about him—maybe even bring some pictures! The only photo I'd ever seen of my dad was a wedding photo of him and Mom. Cassie and I had sneaked into her room years ago and found it. Only once, though. The next time we'd looked for it, it was gone.

Closing my eyes as I walked, I brought up the memory of that faded old photo. Our father had had a kind, handsome face and sandy hair. He'd had his arm around Mom, and both of them had looked amazingly happy. Adorable, even. But it was sad, too, considering how little time they'd had together. Not to mention Cass and me not getting to know him at all . . .

"Ow!" Bianca squawked.

My eyes flew open as I realized I'd walked right into her. She and Liam had stopped near our home-room door to let someone else go past.

"Sorry," I mumbled.

But my friends were already hurrying into the room. I followed.

"Caitlyn Waters!" a voice rang out.

It was my homeroom teacher, Ms. Xavier. She rushed toward me, boho skirt swinging and multiple bracelets clanking. Her expression was always pretty happy, but right now she looked as if she'd just won the lottery.

Then again, if that was the case I doubted she'd show up for school. Lottery or not, I was a little surprised to see her there already. Usually she breezed in right before the bell, which was still almost five minutes away.

"Um, hi." The weekend had been so crazy that I'd almost forgotten about the research project. In addition to being my homeroom teacher, Ms. X taught social studies. We were supposed to come up with a topic involving some aspect of US history, society, or culture and do a paper and oral report. And for some reason, Ms. X had decided that Cassie and I should team up to do our project about being twins. Or famous twins in history. Or something like that. To be honest, I hadn't paid that much attention. I'd had other stuff on my mind.

"Excuse me," the teacher told my friends. "I need

to borrow Caitlyn for a moment."

She grabbed my arm and dragged me toward the corner of the room. At least I think that's what she was doing. Because another vision hit me like a hurricane.

Ms. Xavier faded out, and a new Ms. Xavier took her place. She was in a dark, spooky room. I mean seriously spooky. The talisman was still around my neck, so things were incredibly vivid and I could see every creepy detail—black walls, drapey dark curtains, shelves full of weird skulls and dried-up stuff and glowing candles.

But I didn't focus much on that. The vision version of Ms. Xavier was lying on a huge stone table in the middle of the room. Her curly reddish-brown hair was spread out around her head like a cloud, and her eyes were closed. Someone in a long, black cloak was bending over her, though I couldn't see his or her face . . .

I gasped with relief as Ms. Xavier finally dropped my arm and the vision disappeared as quickly as it had come. The teacher was glancing around the room so she didn't notice my reaction.

By the time she turned to face me, I'd managed to get ahold of myself. Mostly, anyway.

"Caitlyn," Ms. Xavier said with a big smile. "Are you and your sister doing anything after school?"

"Um . . ." My mind flashed to Grandmother Lockwood.

"Good, good." Ms. Xavier seemed to take that as a no. "Because I have something very important to discuss with the two of you. Please meet me here right after the final bell."

"Is this about the project?" I managed to ask, trying not to guess what that cloaked figure was about to do to her in that vision.

She smiled and put her finger to her lips. "After school," she said. "We'll talk then." She winked and hurried over to her desk as she called the class to order.

I watched her go, feeling troubled. Oh, not because of the project—Cassie and I would just have to deal with that. We'd already told her we didn't want to do the twins thing, but Ms. Xavier didn't seem to be getting the message. Maybe it was time to get blunt. Cassie was good at that.

In the meantime, though, I was worried about that vision. Ms. Xavier was into some wacky stuff, but whatever was going on there was downright scary. My friends had told me she was originally from New Orleans, and had tried to teach a unit on voodoo once before the school board had put a stop to it.

Was that what she was doing in my vision? Some kind of voodoo demonstration for our class? No, I was pretty sure that spooky room wasn't anywhere in Aura Middle School. So what was going on?

The PA system crackled to life, startling me. I hurried over and slid into my seat between Liam and Bianca as the morning announcements started.

The first one was about the sixth-grade trip. "Sign-up sheets will be in the office beginning at lunchtime today," the school secretary said. "Please sign up with a partner as soon as possible. Anyone who hasn't paired off by the end of day on Friday will be assigned a partner by the office."

"A partner?" I whispered to my friends.

Bianca nodded. "This school loves the buddy system."

"Yeah." Liam leaned closer. "I wonder if they'd let us sign up as a threesome instead of a duo." He laughed softly. "We could petition the administration and see."

Bianca gave me a sidelong glance. "Sure," she said. "But Caitlyn might want to pair up with her sister."

"Oh, yeah, I didn't think of that." Liam smiled at me. "What do you think, Caitlyn?"

I'd barely heard what they'd said. I was watching Ms. Xavier, who was perched on the edge of her desk just a few feet away.

At that moment I caught her eye, and she gave me a big wink. I gulped and looked away quickly. She was acting weirder than usual. Given how weird the rest of my life was at the moment, I didn't like it.

"Earth to Cait!" Liam poked me in the shoulder.

"Huh?" I blinked at him. "What? Sorry, spaced out."

He chuckled. "Class trip?" he said. "You and your twin?"

I didn't know what he was talking about, though his mention of twins made me shoot another look at Ms. Xavier. Luckily the announcements ended at that moment, and a second later homeroom was over.

Saved by the bell, I thought as my friends gathered up their stuff. With one last troubled glance at Ms. Xavier, I followed them out of the room.

5

CASSIE

"DID YOU HEAR about Sakiko Star?" Lavender said as she dropped her lunch tray on our usual table.

I sat down across from her and poked at the mystery meat on my own tray. Totally gross, as usual. "What about her?"

"Hold on, Megs will want to hear this, too." Lav glanced toward the lunch line.

Megan was heading our way, flanked by two more of our friends. My secret nickname for Abby and Emily was the Minions, mostly because they seemed to worship the ground Megan walked on.

Nice enough girls, just not really strong personality types, if you know what I mean.

"Oh my gosh," Abby exclaimed, throwing herself into the seat next to Lavender. "Did you guys hear the latest about Sakiko?"

Lavender frowned at her. "I was about to tell y'all about that," she said sharply.

I almost rolled my eyes. I'd only been friends with these guys a short time, but I already knew that Lavender Adams hates getting scooped. Hates it like poison. Whatever gossip she'd heard about everyone's favorite pop star, she wanted to be the one to share it first.

"Oh!" Abby's eyes widened. "Sorry, Lav. Go ahead."

Lavender shrugged, still looking sort of disgruntled. "It's no biggie, actually," she said. "She's feuding with that wacky neighbor of hers again."

Megan laughed as she unwrapped her straw. "So what else is new? Ever since Sakiko bought that place in LA it's been one problem after another with that guy."

"I know." Emily slurped her applesauce loudly.

"But the latest pictures are hilarious. She dumped trash all over his yard!"

I laughed along with the others, though I couldn't work up much excitement over celebrity gossip at the moment. Yeah, Sakiko Star was probably my favorite singer of all time. And yeah, the kooky old guy who lived next to her mansion was always doing something crazy, like calling the cops about her gardener weeding too close to the property line or letting his pet parrot squawk outside her window all night. But right now, whatever was going on with them couldn't even hold a candle to my own crazy life.

"Hey, Cassie, you have an eyelash," Emily said suddenly, pulling me away from my thoughts. She leaned closer. "Here, I'll get it." She poked my cheek right below one eye.

The vision was short but super vivid. Emily was lying on a stretcher surrounded by EMTs. At least I was pretty sure it was Emily on the stretcher. I could only see her legs. But I recognized the shoes she was wearing. Besides, it had to be her. She was the only one touching me, and I couldn't see her anywhere else in the scene.

But I could see a bunch of other people, including most of my friends, the B Boys, and more. Actually I could see every detail of the scene—Abby's smudged lip gloss, a poster about the class trip tacked to the wall, somebody's skateboard lying upside down on the floor, various backpacks and purses thrown wherever. I could also see the fear and shock on everyone's faces as they watched the EMTs rush the stretcher out toward a waiting ambulance.

"Cassie?"

I blinked, realizing everyone was staring at me. Oops. Getting those visions always made me go all spacey for a bit. Especially when I was wearing the talisman, which I hated to do. If I was going to see bad things anyway, why make it worse?

Thanks a lot, Cait, I thought, stopping myself from reaching up to touch the key-shaped pendant. My sister had caught up to me in the hall right after homeroom, looking freaked out. Before I could ask what was wrong she'd pressed it into my hand, muttering "We need to talk" before dashing off. Drama much?

Talisman or no talisman, what Grandmother

Lockwood had told us seemed to be true. The visions were getting more frequent and more intense.

"Sorry," I told my friends, forcing a laugh. "The fumes from the mystery meat just overcame me for a sec. What were you guys saying?"

They still looked confused. But just then Lav let out a squeal.

"Here comes Biff," she said, quickly checking her hair. "I bet he picks me."

For a moment I didn't know what she was talking about. Then I remembered: Truth or Dare.

Sure enough, Biff was finally ready for his big announcement. I tried to look like I cared as he pointed playfully from one person to the next, pretending to ponder his choice deeply. Yeah, right. Biff was about as deep as a puddle, which was probably why Lavender had recently decided she had a crush on him.

Speaking of crushes . . . My eyes slipped over to Brayden. He was leaning on his crutches, a small smile on his face as he waited to hear his friend's pick. Then he glanced over, catching me staring.

Oops. I shifted my gaze quickly, hoping I wasn't

blushing. I still wasn't sure exactly how I felt about Brayden. Were we friends? Or maybe more?

Either way, I hated looking like a dork. So I pretended to be fascinated as Biff finally pointed to Lavender.

"Lav, you're up," he said. "Truth or dare."

Lavender did her best to play it cool, even though she'd been practically turning herself inside out trying to get him to notice her. "Oh, I don't know," she said with a shrug. "Truth, I guess."

I traded a glance with Megan, who looked amused. She was probably thinking the same thing I was. Lav wanted Biff to ask her if she had a crush on anyone in the room, or who she thought was the cutest guy on the football team. Something like that.

Unfortunately, Biff wasn't on the same wavelength. "Truth?" he said, sounding disappointed. "Are you sure?"

"Uh-huh." Lav fluttered her eyelashes. "Ask me anything."

"Okay." You could almost see the little wheels turning in Biff's head as he tried to think of a question. Suddenly he grinned. "Got it," he said. "Tell the truth: When was the last time you pooped?"

Lavender looked horrified. "What?" she said with a squawk. "That's not a real question."

"Why not?" Brent guffawed. "It's got a question mark on the end, and everything."

"Yeah," Buzz added. "Sounds like a question to me."

Lavender frowned and crossed her arms over her chest. "No way," she said. "Ask me something else."

"Sure you don't want to choose dare instead?" Biff looked hopeful.

She hesitated, looking tempted. But I could pretty much see her wheels turning, too. After that poop question, she probably wasn't holding out much hope for a super-romantic dare.

"No," she said firmly. "Truth. But something real, not, you know, toilet related."

"Whatever." Biff seemed to be losing interest. "Uh, okay, here's your question. If you were a super-hero, what superpower would you want?"

Lavender wrinkled her nose. "*That's* your new question?"

"Tell the truth, Lav," Minion Abby said with a

giggle. "X-ray vision, or shooting lightning bolts out of your hands?"

"Neither." Lavender rolled her eyes. "I guess I'd want the power to fly."

"That's a good one," Brayden said. "Okay, Lav. Your turn to pick someone."

"Oh, that's right." Suddenly she was interested again. "Okay, Biff—truth or dare?"

"No way," Buzz protested. "You can't ask the person who just asked you."

"Says who?" Lavender retorted.

"Says the rules." Biff shrugged. "Sorry, but my brother said so. It's so you can't just, like, get back at the person who just burned you, you know?" He grinned. "Otherwise I would've made my brother do something awful for sticking me with all those chores."

Brayden nodded. "Yeah. You can pick the person if you get another turn later, but not right after they picked you."

"This game is stupid," Lavender muttered. "But fine. Brayden—truth or dare?"

She smiled at me, smugly, and I gulped, suddenly

nervous. I hadn't actually told Lav that I might be interested in Brayden, but Megan knew. Had she said something?

"Dare." Brayden gestured to his crutches. "Just don't ask me to climb on the school roof or something, okay?"

Lav laughed. "Don't worry, no climbing," she said. "I dare you to kiss someone in this cafeteria."

I froze as several pairs of eyes turned toward me. Brayden's weren't among them; he was staring straight at Lavender. Was he blushing?

"Go, loverboy!" Brent hooted, while Biff and Buzz started making loud smooching sounds.

Brayden swallowed hard, then turned. My hands went all clammy and my heart was pounding. Suddenly I wished I wasn't wearing the talisman. What if he tried to kiss me, and I got a vision?

That and all sorts of other crazy thoughts tumbled through my head. But then I noticed that Brayden wasn't looking at me. He was peering around the caf.

"Aha," he said. Swinging into motion, he headed away from our table. He was getting pretty good on those crutches. Within a few seconds he'd caught up with Velma, everyone's favorite tiny human prune of a cafeteria lady, who was at least a thousand years old and twice as sweet as Maw Maw Jean's pecan pie. As we all watched, he planted a big kiss right on top of her head. A smile lit up Velma's face, and she reached up to pinch Brayden's cheek.

"Aww!" Minion Emily exclaimed. "Too cute."

"Totally," I agreed, though I couldn't help a twinge of disappointment.

When Brayden came back, his friends high-fived him. "Your turn, bro," Buzz said. "Pick someone."

I held my breath as he looked around. If he liked me like Megan said, this was his chance. Would he choose me?

Just as he turned my way, my sister dashed over. "Cassie!" she exclaimed breathlessly. "I've been looking everywhere for you."

"What?" I was distracted, still watching Brayden. "Where else would I be?"

She grabbed my arm. "Come on," she said. "We need to talk." Suddenly seeming to notice all my friends staring at her, she gave them a weak smile. "Uh, twin business. You know."

Ugh. Talk about bad timing! Then again, Caitlyn had always been the queen of that. Not sure what else to do, I allowed her to drag me away.

Soon we were huddled behind the trash bins. "I thought I should warn you before you head off to social studies, Ms. Xavier is going to talk to you about staying after school today. She already said something to me in homeroom."

"She did?" I glanced over at my table. Brayden had chosen Brent. At least I assumed that was why Brent was stuffing everyone's mystery meat into his mouth, including mine. No loss there.

"Yes," Cait said. "And she seemed really intense about it, too. I couldn't say no."

I tuned back in. "You told her we'd come? Today?" I exclaimed. "In case you forgot, we already have something going on after school. And we already won't have much time, since Mom leaves for work at four."

"I know. But she wouldn't take no for an answer." Caitlyn stared at me. "Do you think she knows there's, you know, something going on with us? Everyone says she's into that kind of stuff."

"What kind of stuff?"

"You know—extrasensory powers, voodoo, crystals, whatever."

I shrugged. "Okay. But she's also really into convincing us to do her stupid twin project idea. I'm sure that's all she wants to talk about. Again."

"Maybe." Cait seemed unconvinced. "But listen, there's more. While I was talking to her, I had a vision. A weird one."

I could tell she was about to launch into a full recap, but I wasn't really in the mood. I wanted to get back over to my table before the B Boys wandered off.

"Me, too," I said, shuddering at the memory of Minion Emily on that stretcher. "We can talk about it later, okay?"

Without giving her a chance to protest, I hurried back to my friends.

As it turned out, my sister was right. Ms. Xavier accosted me as soon as I walked into social studies about staying after school, yakkity yak. I just nodded. What choice did I have? With any luck we could get in and out of there fast and still get home before Grandmother Lockwood turned up.

"Good, good." The teacher beamed at me. "You know, Cassie, I almost feel as if you already knew what I was going to say. Did Caitlyn mention my request, or is it just twintuition?"

She winked, and I froze. Twintuition? That was what Cait and I used to call it when we tried to read each other's minds when we were younger. Maybe it wasn't a stretch that someone else might come up with the same term. But why was she using it now?

What if she does know something? I wondered, going hot and cold at the thought.

Then Brayden swung into the room, and I shook it off. Ms. Xavier was a loon. Period, full stop. There was no way she knew anything.

Besides, between wondering how to convince my grandmother to tell us anything useful and figuring out how I really felt about Brayden, I had much more important stuff to worry about than what the kookiest teacher in school had on her mind.

6
CAITLYN

AS SOON AS my last class let out, I dumped my stuff in my locker and went to find Cassie. She wasn't at her locker, or Megan's, either. Finally I tracked her down at her friend Emily's. Bianca's locker was a few doors down, and she and Liam were standing there.

"Hey, Caitlyn," Liam said with a smile as I charged past. "We were just talking about the school trip again. Do you want to—"

"Sorry, can't talk now," I told him breathlessly, barely slowing down.

I felt bad for blowing them off. But I didn't want to waste any time. Grandmother Lockwood had promised to contact us before four o'clock, and we still had to talk to Ms. Xavier before we could go home.

Cassie saw me coming and said something to her friends. She stepped out to meet me.

"Ready to go?" she said. "I want to get home and see if . . ." She glanced around. "You know."

"Me, too," I said. "But first we have that meeting with Ms. X. Remember?"

By the annoyed expression on her face, I guessed she'd forgotten. "Right," she muttered. "Let's get this over with."

She stomped off down the hall without waiting to see if I was following. I caught up with her outside the classroom door. Ms. Xavier was inside, leaning on her desk and talking to some seventh grader. But when she saw us in the doorway, she quickly ushered the other kid out.

"Come in, girls. Come in," the teacher said, closing the door after us. "Have a seat."

I started to obey, but Cassie grabbed my hand to stop me. "That's okay," she said firmly. "We can't stay—our mom is expecting us home."

"All right then." Ms. Xavier seemed unfazed. She stepped a little closer, clasping her hands excitedly. "This won't take too long."

"O-okay." Cassie sounded funny. When I glanced over, she looked as if she'd suddenly come down with a bad case of indigestion.

Catching me looking, she mouthed a single word at me: *vision.*

I had no idea what that was about; she wasn't touching anyone so that couldn't be possible. But I couldn't exactly ask her what she meant in front of Ms. Xavier. Luckily the teacher was staring into space and hadn't noticed anything.

Suddenly she clapped her hands and stared at us. "Well, girls," she said with a smile. "I always suspected there was something . . . special about you two."

I gulped. "Special? You mean being twins?"

She laughed heartily. "Yes, that was my first

clue." She winked. "But I've always had a bit of extrasensory power myself, and I felt an unusual energy coming from the two of you from the start. That was why I wanted you to do the twin study for your research project."

I relaxed. Cassie was right—this was just more of the same.

But her next words tensed me right back up again, tighter than a cowboy's jeans. "So of course, I was thrilled when Mr. Campbell confirmed my theory."

"Mr. Campbell?" Cassie echoed slowly.

The teacher beamed at her. "Gabriel Campbell, from your sister's section."

"Yeah, I know him." Cassie shot me a worried look. "What does he have to do with us?"

"It seems he heard you two talking about this special vision you have," Ms. Xavier said. "Something about touching each other and seeing things that aren't there? And reading each other's minds?"

It sounded as if Gabe hadn't overheard everything—just enough to jump to conclusions, however wrong they were. But still, my heart pounded, and I tried to stay calm.

"Oh, I'm sure he was just joking with you," I said.

"No, he was quite serious—and quite certain about what he heard. He said you two sounded as if you were struggling to handle what you were seeing, and he was very concerned about you."

"Yeah, right," Cassie muttered.

Ms. Xavier didn't seem to hear her. "Knowing of my affinity for all things paranormal, he came to me." She squeezed my shoulder. "And of course, I'm happy to help."

I opened my mouth to tell her that Gabe was making the whole thing up. But the words never came. Because my head was buzzing and the teacher smiling down at me was fading out.

Cassie was still wearing the talisman, so the vision wasn't as vivid as the earlier one. It wasn't as scary, either. Ms. Xavier was right there in her classroom, handing something to Megan March while glancing at the empty desk in front of her, which was decorated with a big green-and-gold ribbon.

Weird. I did my best to shake it off as soon as Ms. Xavier let go of me. But it was too late. She was staring at me intently.

"Did you just have one?" she exclaimed. "A vision thingy? You looked so odd there for a moment . . ."

"N-no," I stammered, shooting Cassie a panicky look. "I was just, um, thinking that your twin project idea might be, um, fun."

I gulped, seeing that Ms. X didn't believe me. It wasn't easy to just snap out of a vision, though, and I guess I was feeling a little confused and didn't sound as convincing as I hoped. In any case, it was too late to take it back now. So I decided to make the best of it.

"But we don't want everyone to know about—about us," I added quickly. "So we wouldn't want to talk about, you know, any of this extra stuff in the oral report."

The teacher rubbed her chin thoughtfully. "Yes, I understand," she said. "Not everyone is as open-minded as I am about such things. I suppose it would be fine if we restricted your oral presentation to twins throughout history, and confined the more interesting parts to the written report."

I could still feel my sister glaring at me. But I forced a smile as Ms. Xavier patted my shoulder, thankfully without bringing on a vision this time. I mean, what was I supposed to do? Almost anyone else probably would've thought Gabe was just making up stories. Or that Cass and I were delusional at the very least. But Ms. Xavier? This was right up her alley, and she seemed totally ready to believe, especially after seeing me have a vision right in front of her . . .

"Can we go now?" Cassie said. "Like I said, our mom's expecting us."

"Of course." Ms. Xavier shooed us toward the door, her bracelets jingling. "We can discuss details tomorrow."

Cassie grabbed my arm and dragged me out of the room. "This is an epic disaster," she muttered as we hurried down the hall. "How could you agree to—"

She stopped short as Gabe Campbell stepped into view just ahead. He was smirking.

"You rat," Cassie spat out. "What's your problem, anyway?"

"I'm not the one with problems," he replied. "You

two are the ones who think you're mind readers or whatever. I just reckoned Ms. Xavier would be the perfect person to tell about it." He laughed. "Especially since y'all seemed so excited about doing your research project on being twins like she wanted."

I glared at him. Obviously he'd overheard even more than we'd feared. Had I talked too loudly about Ms. Xavier's project idea in homeroom? Or had he skulked around Cassie's lunch table and heard her complaining about it to her friends?

Either way, he'd figured out the perfect way to get at us. He knew the last thing we wanted to do was that crazy twins project, and that Ms. Xavier would believe what he'd overheard about the Sight even if he thought we were lying or crazy. Cassie was glaring at him, her fingers twitching. My twintuition couldn't tell me whether she was considering punching him or strangling him, but it was working well enough to know we should get out of there, pronto.

"Come on," I said, yanking her past Gabe. "We don't have time for this."

The weather was finally cooling off a little, and a breeze tickled my face as we stepped outside and turned toward home. "We need to figure out what to do about this," Cassie said grimly.

"What can we do? We'll have to play along, I guess." I shrugged.

"And then what?" She kicked at a stone on the sidewalk. "Wait for her to blab to someone about our superduper twin powers? You can't possibly believe she's actually going to be able to keep this to herself." She shook her head. "I should have guessed that stupid vision was something terrible," she muttered.

"What vision? The one you had today?" I realized we hadn't shared our latest visions yet.

"No." She glanced over at me. "A while back, I saw the two of us talking to Ms. X in her classroom."

"Oh, right." That must have been what she was referring to when we were with Ms. Xavier before. She'd told me about that one, but it hadn't seemed important at the time. "So today it came true?"

"Bingo. Another neutral vision turns out to be bad."

"Okay, but get this," I said. "The good-bad thing might be changing, for real. Because I had a vision today that seemed super creepy . . ."

I filled her in on my homeroom vision about Ms. Xavier.

She listened with interest. "That's the one you had just now?" she said. "When she almost caught you?"

"Oh. Actually, no—I had the creepy skull room one this morning. The one I had just now was nothing important."

"Are you sure?" She shifted her book bag to her other shoulder as we paused to look both ways before crossing the street. "Because I would've said the same thing about the one we just lived out."

"Right." She had a point, so I described the vision with Ms. Xavier and Megan as thoroughly as I could.

"A ribbon?" Cassie interrupted when I got to that part. "And which desk was it on?"

"The one right in front of Megan's," I said. "There

was nobody sitting there."

"That's Emily's seat." Cassie frowned. "Weird."

"Why?" I shrugged. "The ribbon was Aura's school colors—green and gold. Maybe it just meant Emily won, like, a cheerleading award or something."

"Yeah, probably," Cassie said slowly. "Only I had a vision about Emily today, too."

She told me about it. "An ambulance? Wow." I thought for a second. "Okay, we should probably try to figure out what's going on with her."

"Right. In all our spare time, when we're not dealing with Ms. X, or our new grandmother, or our freaked-out mom, or—"

"Okay, okay," I broke in. "I hear you. But still, if Emily's going to end up in an ambulance, we should probably try to stop it from happening."

"Yeah."

Just then I heard someone calling my name. Turning, I saw Liam racing after us, his backpack flopping against his back.

"Oh, great," Cassie muttered. "Geek, incoming."

"Hush!" I warned. Then I pasted a smile onto my

face as my friend caught up to us. "Hey, Liam."

"I can't believe I ran into you," he exclaimed breathlessly. "I thought everybody'd be gone by the time I got out of the student council meeting."

"We had to stop in and talk to Ms. Xavier about our social studies project," I told him.

Cassie was already walking again. I followed, and Liam fell into step beside me. "Did you guys hear about this Truth or Dare thing?" he asked eagerly. "Everyone at the meeting was talking about it!"

"Yeah, I guess." I wasn't paying much attention to the Truth or Dare craze, though a few people in my afternoon classes had been all atwitter about it.

Liam grinned. "It's spreading fast," he said. "There are like five or six different sets of dares going right now."

"Really?" I said. "How'd that happen? I thought people were getting picked one at a time."

"Someone told me that all the guys in their art elective were dared to come to class without shirts on, and then each of those people got to choose someone after they did it."

"Yeah, I was there for that." Cassie grinned. "It took Mrs. Ortega, like, ten minutes to notice. Megan got pictures on her phone. Epic."

"Anyway, I want to be ready in case someone chooses me tomorrow," Liam said. "I'm going to make a list of dares and truth questions I can use." He shrugged. "Bianca already warned me not to pick her, so I'm planning to try to really get Josh and Goober."

"Good idea," I said, smiling briefly in spite of my distraction. Liam's friends Josh and Goober were in the other section, so I didn't know them that well, but the three of them loved to goof around together. I was just glad that Liam didn't seem to be targeting me. "Good luck."

"Wait," he said. "Will you help me come up with ideas? I want to make sure I have some really good stuff ready."

Normally that sort of thing would have sounded like a lot of fun. But today I wasn't in the mood. Besides, Grandmother Lockwood could be waiting at our house right now. "Sorry, I can't right now," I said. "Um, rain check?"

"But I want to be ready tomorrow." He sounded disappointed. "Are you sure you can't do it now?"

"You heard her, dude." Cassie grabbed my hand and pulled me along faster. "We've got to go. Like, now."

"Oh. Okay." He stopped, watching us hurry on ahead.

"Sorry!" I called over my shoulder, meaning it. And hating that I couldn't tell him why I was too busy to hang out. If Cassie had given me half a second, maybe at least I could've told him our grandmother was in town. That would have explained things well enough.

Oh well. Maybe someday soon I'd be able to tell him everything. But first I needed to find out more myself.

"Come on," I told Cass, putting on another burst of speed. "Let's get home and see if Grandmother Lockwood is there yet."

7

CASSIE

WHEN CAITLYN AND I clattered into the house, Mom was in the living room paying bills at her desk. "Is she here?" I blurted out.

Mom looked up, knowing immediately who we were talking about. "Nope, haven't heard a peep from your grandmother all day."

She didn't sound super bummed. In fact, I was pretty sure she was trying not to look smug about Grandmother Lockwood's silence.

Whatever. I dropped my bag on the bench by the

door, then flopped on the sofa. It wasn't as hot out as it had been lately, but that fast walk home had been enough to wear me out. Not to mention the super-stressful meeting with Ms. Xavier.

Which reminded me. How could Caitlyn have agreed to do that stupid twins project? Was she crazy? We needed to have a serious talk about how to handle this. Maybe there was still time to convince Ms. X that Gabe had made the whole thing up, or . . .

"We could try calling her," Caitlyn was saying, which dragged me out of my thoughts.

"Who? Granny L?" I said. "Good idea. What's her number?"

Cait shrugged and glanced at Mom. "Do you have it?"

"I don't think your grandmother is the type of person who carries a cell phone around with her everywhere." Mom checked her watch. "I need to get dressed for work. I leave in less than an hour."

Once again, smug. And it was easy to guess why. Mom had made Grandmother Lockwood promise to get in touch before she had to leave at four. Which didn't give her much time to get here if we wanted to have any time to talk before Mom had to take off.

I felt helpless and annoyed. Why was everything going wrong all of a sudden?

My phone buzzed. It was a group text from Lavender, forwarding some photos of Sakiko Star picking up tin cans off her lawn. I glanced at it, but my gaze caught on Emily's name in the list of recipients. With a shudder, I flashed back to the vision I'd had of her on the stretcher. Cait and I had seen scary stuff like that before. For instance, Caitlyn had recently had a vision of Liam bleeding all over the place at our pool party.

That one turned out to be nothing very bad, though, I reminded myself as I clicked off my phone. *Of course, that's probably because it was Happy Shiny Caitlyn's vision and not mine.*

That reminded me of Grandmother Lockwood's surprised reaction when we'd told her about our visions being split into good and bad. It made me wonder exactly how much she could actually tell us about our weirdo power. She'd pretty much said that nobody knew a lot about the Sight.

Caitlyn wandered in from the kitchen, slurping from a glass of sweet tea. "Want to talk?" she asked with a cautious glance toward Mom's room. "If Grandmother Lockwood isn't going to show today . . ."

"She still has time." I checked my watch and grimaced. Forty minutes and counting.

Caitlyn sat down beside me, grabbing a coaster for her drink. "We could try calling her hotel," she said. "I'm sure we can get the number from information and just ask the front desk to put us through."

"What's the point?" I leaned back and stared at the ceiling. "Six Oaks is at least twenty minutes away." Hopping to my feet, I headed over to grab my bag. "Guess I'll get started on my homework."

Thirty-five minutes later, Mom stuck her head into my room. "I'm heading out in a sec," she said. "Dinner's in the fridge."

"Okay." I got up and stretched, ready for a snack.

As I followed Mom out into the narrow hall, the

doorbell rang. Mom glanced back.

"Expecting someone?" she asked.

"Not anymore," I said, following Mom to the door.

I reached the living room just as Grandmother Lockwood stepped in, dressed in a tidy blue suit and pearls.

"Verity!" Mom snapped. "We were expecting you earlier."

"You told me to be here before four." Grandmother Lockwood's cool gray eyes swept over Mom's uniform. "I intended to arrive earlier, but I was delayed. No matter, though—it's not four just yet, mmm?"

"Technically, she's right," I said. "It's like three of."

Mom sputtered. "That's not what I— This is unacceptable! You'll have to come back another time."

"What?" Caitlyn wailed. "Mom, no!"

"You can't send her away!" I added.

"Oh, can't I?" Mom was sliding dangerously

close to scarymama territory.

I opened my mouth to argue, but Caitlyn shot me a look. "Please, Mom," she said softly. "She's our grandmother, and we want to get to know her while she's here. You've always told us that family is important."

That was something Mom liked to say, especially whenever she made us eat Aunt Cheryl's disgusting green bean casserole. She glowered at all of us, I guess not knowing how to respond to that.

"What do you think is going to happen, Deidre?" Grandmother Lockwood said. "I'm not going to do anything cruel or unusual to these girls. I promise." A half smile played around the corners of her mouth.

Mom didn't look amused. "One can only imagine," she shot back. "John told me the family history."

What did that mean? I traded a confused look with my sister.

"We're just going to talk, Mama," Cait pleaded in her best goody-two-shoes peacemaker voice. "Promise!"

"Yeah, me, too," I put in, trying to imitate her

tone and sickly-sweet smile.

Mom sneaked a peek at her watch. "All right," she said at last, though she still sounded annoyed. "I reckon there's no harm in talking. But don't leave this house until I get back."

Caitlyn and I quickly crossed our hearts. With one last glare at Grandmother Lockwood, Mom hurried out.

"Well, then." Grandmother Lockwood stepped out of the doorway and took a seat at the dining table. "Let's get started."

Caitlyn and I wandered toward her. "Get started?" Cait echoed.

Grandmother Lockwood dug into her large beige purse. "Yes," she said. "I thought we'd talk a bit more, and then—"

I gasped, not hearing the rest as she pulled out a battered leather-bound book. "The diary!" I blurted out. "I thought we'd never see it again."

She set the little book on the table. "I'm returning it to you. I wanted you to have it, or I wouldn't have sent it to you in the first place."

"Is this the same diary the message board was talking about?" Cait asked. "The one some guy posted about finding in a secondhand shop?"

"One and the same." Grandmother Lockwood glanced at the diary, looking slightly peeved. "I can't imagine how it ended up out of our family's possession. In fact, it's rather lucky that you stumbled upon that site, Caitlyn. Otherwise we might not have realized it wasn't with your father's old things anymore."

"How did you get it back?" I asked.

Grandmother Lockwood shrugged, and for a second I thought she wasn't going to answer. "It doesn't matter," she said at last. "The important thing is that it's safe."

I didn't think that was much of an answer. But I had more important questions in mind just then.

"So what's it say?" I asked, reaching for the diary.

Cait grabbed it at the same time. Our hands brushed each other as we both touched the soft leather cover.

Then I gasped, instantly overwhelmed by the strongest vision yet. I'd been looking at Cait and

I could still see her, her eyes wide and her mouth forming a little O of surprise. But she was so faint she might as well have been a ghost.

And this time, there was no brighter, more vivid Caitlyn to replace her. Instead, I saw a sunny outdoor scene. Cait and our grandmother were nowhere in sight. The only person there was a tall, skinny man with a long black braid. He was dressed in jeans and a dark shirt with a camera around his neck. But he wasn't taking pictures—instead he was digging around in a large trash can sitting on the sidewalk in front of a tall hedge. Weird! As I watched, he straightened up, peering at something in his hand. I couldn't quite see what it was, except that it was pretty small and glinted in the bright sunshine . . .

"Whoa!" I gulped as I staggered back, breaking contact with Cait and the diary. "That was intense!"

"Did you each have a vision?" Grandmother Lockwood demanded eagerly, leaning forward.

I blinked at Cait, realizing she looked as stunned as I felt. "Yeah," she managed to say. "It was a strange one."

"Mine, too." With a shaky hand, I pulled out a chair and dropped onto it. "I mean, there wasn't even anyone I knew in it this time!"

Grandmother Lockwood's eyes were sharp. "Tell me."

So I did, describing the scene I'd just witnessed. About ten words in, Caitlyn started nodding.

"I saw the same thing," she said when I'd finished. "I didn't recognize the man either."

"Or the street," I added. "It wasn't anywhere in Aura, at least I'm pretty sure it wasn't. The trash cans looked different from the ones here."

Our grandmother drummed her fingers on the table. "This man," she said. "Tell me again what he looked like. Everything you can remember."

I shrugged. "Skinny, tall, boring clothes. He was white or maybe Latino, with a long, dark hippie braid down his back. But he wasn't old enough to be a real hippie like our great-uncle Vern, probably only thirty or so. Camera around his neck."

"Not just any old camera," Caitlyn put in. "It was a serious-looking one with a big lens. Like you see nature photographers and people like that using."

"And you didn't see anyone else?" Grandmother Lockwood prompted. "Nobody you knew, perhaps in the background?"

"Nope," I said. "Trust me, the whole scene is totally seared into my brain. There was nobody else there."

Cait nodded. "That's different from any visions we've had before," she said with a glance at me. "I mean, up until now we always saw the person we were touching."

"Yeah." I turned to our grandmother. "How weird is that? I mean, does it happen a lot?"

She cleared her throat. "It's not unheard of."

That didn't seem like much of an answer to me, especially paired with the surprised expression on her face when she'd heard about our vision. Once again I found myself wondering how much she really knew about the Sight.

"In any case," she went on before we could ask more questions. "We need to work out exactly where you girls are in the evolution of your powers, and how much you know about what you're experiencing. Normally you would have been learning about the Sight since you were old enough to understand, preparing yourself just in case you were the one who ended up with it. The whole family would then help guide you through the transition into your full powers."

"Yeah." I frowned. "Thanks to Mom, this is all pretty much brand new."

Verity sighed, her stern expression softening. "Don't blame your mother too much," she said. "She was probably hoping someone else in your generation would be the Seer. That would have been much easier for her, especially after what happened to your father."

I held my breath. Was she about to tell us—finally—how our dad had died? And whether the Sight had caused it? "What did happen to him?" I asked.

Instantly, the stern face was back. "We'll begin the testing right now," she said. "There's clearly no time to lose."

8
CAITLYN

I WAS SO distracted by Grandmother Lockwood's mention of our dad that it took a second for the rest to sink in. "Wait," I blurted out. "Testing? That doesn't sound like something Mom would want us to do without her."

Cassie rolled her eyes. "Get real, Caitlyn," she said. "She knew we'd be talking about the visions. I'm sure this is just part of that."

"Yes, but—"

"Your sister is right." Grandmother Lockwood's

voice was crisp and final. "What I have in mind for today is little more than talking in any case. Let's begin by going over all the visions you've had so far."

I had to admit, that didn't sound too bad. "Okay," I said. "I'll start. My first one was with Mom . . ."

Grandmother Lockwood listened intently as Cassie and I described our visions, taking turns to keep them mostly in chronological order. She didn't say a word until I got to one I'd had a while back of Mom holding hands with some guy I didn't know with holiday decorations in the background.

"This man," Grandmother Lockwood interrupted. "Is it the same one you saw in your vision today?"

"No," I said. "He didn't look anything like that." I hesitated, shooting Cassie a glance. "Actually, the guy in the Christmas vision looked sort of like an older version of our dad."

Our grandmother's eyebrows shot up. "What do you mean?"

"We saw their wedding photo once," Cassie put in. "Sandy hair, kind of square chin, nice blue eyes."

"Yes." Grandmother Lockwood stared at me,

looking a bit shaken. "And this man with your mother—he looked like John?"

"Well, not exactly," I said quickly, not wanting to freak her out. As hard as it was for us that our father had died so young, Cassie and I had never really known him. But our grandmother had lost the son she'd raised and loved. That had to be even tougher. "I mean, he was older, for one thing. And his hair was shorter than in that photo and maybe a little lighter, and his face was paler, too."

"Yeah, we figure Mom must have a type," Cassie said. "Guess this means she's going to start dating again. She'd better hurry, though—Christmas is only a couple of months away."

I nodded. "Unless maybe I was seeing next Christmas," I suggested. "How far ahead can the visions be, anyway?"

Grandmother Lockwood didn't respond. She didn't even seem to hear me. She was staring into space, looking vaguely perplexed.

"What?" Cassie said. "Is something wrong?"

"No, not at all." She blinked, glancing at us. "Go on. Next vision?"

I traded a look with my sister. She was frowning, and my twintuition said she was getting fed up with the way our grandmother kept asking questions but not answering any of ours. I knew how she felt, but I didn't want to make Grandmother Lockwood mad. Not now, when we might finally be getting somewhere.

"Okay," I said quickly. "I think my next one was about my friend Bianca . . ."

Once again, Grandmother Lockwood kept quiet for a spell while we talked. Then Cassie got to her vision of the two of us in the empty classroom with Ms. Xavier.

"That one came true today," Cassie said after describing the vision. "Turns out she's onto us, thanks to Greasy Gabe."

We'd already talked about Gabe because of some earlier visions involving him. So Grandmother Lockwood didn't react to the nickname. But she leaned forward.

"Onto you?" she said. "What do you mean by that?"

I shrugged. "I guess Gabe heard us talking about

the Sight," I admitted. "He knows Ms. X is into that kind of thing—you know, paranormal stuff, voodoo, anything alternative, I guess."

"Yeah. So he spilled the beans so Ms. X would make our lives miserable." Cassie made a face. "Any other teacher probably would have laughed it off if Gabe told them, or they would've had us committed, but not wackadoodle Ms. X. She wants to make us her personal pet project."

"Hold on." Grandmother Lockwood's voice was dangerously cold. "Are you telling me this teacher of yours knows about the Sight?"

"Sort of. Or she thinks she does." I gulped, not liking the stormy look on her face. "But it's okay, everyone knows she's kind of out there. Besides, she promised not to tell anyone, not that anyone would believe her if she did."

"I see." Grandmother Lockwood stood abruptly, her gray eyes flashing fire. "I can't believe you girls were so careless. In all the years of the Lockwood legacy, this has never happened before. We've always kept family business within the family."

Cassie rolled her eyes. "Whatever. It's not like

we did it on purpose."

"It doesn't matter. It was stupid."

She was glaring at us as if we were the worst people in the world. I couldn't believe it. Talk about unfair!

I don't get mad that often, but I could feel a slow burn starting inside me right then. "We had no idea what was happening to us, remember?" I said, my voice shaking a little. "It took a while for us even to realize it was happening to both of us. So sue us if we want to talk about it once in a while!"

"You shouldn't have spoken in front of others." Her voice dripped ice.

"We didn't!" I cried. "Aren't you listening? We made a mistake—we know that now. But we took precautions. We went off by ourselves to an empty classroom. It's not like we knew Gabe was out there." I glared at her. "Anyway, who else are we supposed to talk to about this besides each other? It's not like you're even telling us anything useful or important!" Out of the corner of my eye I could see Cassie making a cutting motion across her throat with one finger, but I didn't care. My whole body was shaking now.

"You won't even tell us how our own father died!"

Pushing my chair away so hard it fell, I raced for the front door, suddenly needing fresh air. The tears were coming fast and I almost tripped down the steps, but caught myself and stomped out to the middle of the yard. Then I stopped, gulping in the humid soup that passes for air in Central Texas. The limo from yesterday was at the curb, and I could see the same driver, Al, napping in the front seat.

Grandmother Lockwood followed me outside. "Listen to me, Caitlyn," she said sternly, shooting a wary look toward the limo. "This is very serious, do you hear me? Whenever outsiders learn of the Sight, bad things tend to happen. Very, very bad things."

"Whoa," Cassie said. "This is it."

Grandmother Lockwood rounded on her. "What?"

"You two." She waved a hand at us. "You were wearing that blue suit, the whole shebang. I already saw this fight in a vision. I just told you about it, like, five minutes ago, remember?"

Grandmother Lockwood stared at her for a moment. Then her shoulders slumped and she let out a sigh. "I'm sorry, Caitlyn," she said. "You're absolutely right. This isn't your fault. Yours either, Cassandra. Let's go back inside." She glanced at the limo, where Al was beginning to stir. I guess even with the windows up and the AC on, we'd been making enough noise to wake him.

We followed her back into the house. I was taking deep breaths, trying to get myself under control. Grandmother Lockwood walked over and picked up the diary.

"So what about Ms. Xavier?" Cassie asked. "Should we tell her we won't do the project after all, or what?"

"Don't worry about that, I'll take care of it." Our grandmother checked her watch, then tucked the diary back in her purse. "Now I'd better be off. I'll be in touch soon."

"Wait!" I cried.

But she was already striding out without a backward glance.

"DO YOU THINK she'll come over again today after school?" I asked. It was Tuesday morning, and we'd just reached the Aura Middle School steps.

Cassie glanced up at the building in front of us. "Your guess is as good as mine. Now let's zip it, okay? It's bad enough that Ms. Xavier knows about us. We don't want the whole school to find out what freaks we are."

I nodded. We'd been discussing Grandmother Lockwood's latest visit the whole walk to school, and we'd pretty much covered it, anyway.

When I stepped into homeroom, a petite young woman with short hair was sitting at Ms. Xavier's desk. She looked only a couple of years older than my cousin Joy, who was in college. "Who's that?" I asked Liam and Bianca, sliding into my seat between them.

"Substitute," Bianca said without looking up from the book she was reading.

"Ms. Xavier's absent today?" I bit my lip, flashing back to the intense look in Grandmother Lockwood's eyes when she'd promised to "take care of" the problem of our social studies project.

But I shook it off, telling myself I was being silly. Ms. Xavier had probably caught a cold or something.

Good. That would give us an extra day to figure out what to do about her.

"I'm glad you're here, Caitlyn," Liam said. "We were just talking about the class trip."

Bianca finally looked up from her book. "You used to live in San Antonio, right?" she said. "Do you know if there are any good music stores there? I'm hoping there will be some free time in the schedule so we can go shopping."

Lavender was just wandering past. She stopped in front of Bianca's desk. "Music stores?" she said. "Are you talking about real music, or, like, dorky marching band music?"

I was surprised she was talking to us at all, let alone in an only slightly obnoxious way. Bianca looked a little startled, too, but she glanced at the clarinet case by her desk and then shrugged. "Either one, I guess," she told Lavender.

"Oh. Because I'm totally going to hit up this shop I saw online called Viral Vinyl," Lavender said eagerly.

"I know that place," I said. "It's right around the corner from where my aunt and uncle live."

"Really?" Lavender's eyes widened. "So you've been there? I heard they have a huge selection of super-rare foreign stuff. Like Sakiko's first album that was only released in Japan!"

"Yeah, it's pretty neat," I began.

Before I could go into detail, the B Boys rushed over to us. Buzz poked Lavender on the shoulder.

"Truth or dare, Lav!" he yelled with a grin.

"Again?" Lavender rolled her eyes, but she was smiling at the same time. She eyed Biff. "I think this time I'll pick dare."

"Cool!" Buzz's eyes lit up. "I dare you to go change into your gym suit and wear it until lunchtime."

He grinned, looking proud of himself. Biff and Brent laughed and high-fived each other behind him.

"What? You can't be serious!" Lavender put a hand on her heart and pretended to stagger back from shock.

"Ow!" I said as she stepped on my foot.

The rest of my complaint caught in my throat as a vision sputtered into view. It was a quick one, and a little fuzzy since I wasn't wearing the talisman. It showed Lavender and Biff kissing on a darkened bus.

Lavender moved off my foot and I snapped out of it immediately. Glancing around, I was relieved to see that nobody had noticed my brief space-out. My friends were laughing along with the B Boys as Lavender loudly proclaimed that she was going to make gym suits so stylish they'd be on the cover of *Vogue* by next week. Or something; I wasn't really paying much attention as I did my best to shake off the vision.

Ew, I thought. *Obviously I just got a sneak preview of the class trip. I so didn't need to see that. Though I suppose it's a good warning not to sit anywhere near those two on the bus . . .*

I grimaced, wondering if this was what Grandmother Lockwood had meant when she'd talked about the visions going into overdrive right after our twelfth birthday. Lavender had barely touched me, but it had caused a vision. How many was that now this week? I tried to recall if Grandmother Lockwood had mentioned how long that extra-intense period usually lasted. Because it was already getting old. For real.

9
CASSIE

"CHECK IT OUT," I said as we rounded the corner onto our block that afternoon. "She's here."

The limo was parked by the curb again. I sped up, Caitlyn at my heels. She waved at Al, who was in the front seat of the car with the window rolled down.

When we neared the front door, the sound of muffled yelling came from inside. "Uh-oh," Caitlyn said. "Sounds like Mom is here, too. And she's not happy."

I shrugged. "What else is new lately?"

They both shut up when we stepped in. "Girls," Grandmother Lockwood said. "I'm glad you're home. We have much to discuss."

I glanced at Mom, who was glowering but silent. "Cool," I said. "Let's discuss, then."

We all sat down at the table. Grandmother Lockwood had her purse with her again. Was the diary in there? She didn't make any move to take it out. Was she keeping it hidden from Mom?

She clasped her hands in front of her. "Today I'd like to fill you in on the history of the Lockwood family. The first known instance of the Sight occurred in a woman called Caroline Elizabeth Lockwood, who was born in the mid-eighteenth century."

She rambled on for a while about various long-dead Lockwoods. I tapped my foot under the table, trying to stay patient.

But what can I say? I'm not a patient person.

"Is this really important right now?" I burst out at last, interrupting her monologue about some guy named Cecil Lockwood. "I mean, shouldn't we be talking more about what's happening with us today?"

Grandmother Lockwood frowned. "I'll thank you not to interrupt, Cassandra."

Just then Mom's phone buzzed. She pulled it out and frowned as she read the text.

"Seriously?" she muttered. Then she looked up. "I got called in for a meeting at work."

"Now?" Caitlyn said in surprise.

Mom shrugged and stood. "Duty calls," she said. "I'll be back as soon as I can."

This time she didn't gripe about us talking to our grandmother without her. I wondered if it had to do with the boring history lesson. Come to think of it, a meeting at the cop shop sounded a lot more exciting than more of that.

As soon as Mom was gone, our grandmother cleared her throat. "All right, girls," she said. "We'll continue with the family history at a later time. Let's move on to other topics."

I sat up, relieved. "Cool," I said. "Cait and I both had visions today we wanted to talk to you about."

"Later," she replied. "I'd like to do some testing

while Deidre isn't here to interfere."

Whoa, okay. Now we were getting somewhere. Glancing over, I saw that Caitlyn seemed alarmed.

"Fine," I said before she could protest. "Let's do it."

"But—" Caitlyn began.

"It'll be fine," I told her. "You're the one who keeps wanting to know how this whole deal works, right?"

"Yeah." She still looked troubled, but she nodded at our grandmother. "Okay. What are we going to do?"

Grandmother Lockwood took the diary out of her purse and asked if we had the talisman. When I pulled it out from under my shirt and showed her, she nodded.

"Good," she said. "I want both of you to touch both items. Make sure you're touching each other, too."

Caitlyn moved over to sit next to me. I pulled off the talisman and held it out so she could grab part of the chain. Then we took each other by the hand, resting our free hands on the diary.

"Now what?" Caitlyn said.

"You're not getting a vision?" our grandmother asked.

I frowned and dropped Cait's hand. "It doesn't work like that," I said. "We can't just call up a vision whenever we want, like ordering a pizza. But you should know that if you're the expert."

She frowned. "I do know that," she said sharply. "But sometimes with the help of a focusing object—"

"A what?" Caitlyn interrupted.

"You mean the diary?" I added.

"Yes, the diary, the talisman, anything else that's been in the possession of a Lockwood with the Sight," she said. "You see, each vision you have adds energy to everything you're touching at the time."

"What do you mean?" Caitlyn asked.

"A vision expends much energy," she said. "That's why most Seers are shaken and confused afterward."

"Yeah, I hear you," I muttered, glancing at Cait.

"Some of that energy seeps into the things you touch—your clothes, jewelry, whatever's in your pockets at the time," Grandmother Lockwood said.

"What about people?" I asked. "Like the ones the visions are about?"

She shrugged. "I suppose them, too," she agreed. "But in objects, it can become concentrated after a while. Then if another vision comes while you're touching that item—"

"It makes the vision stronger"—now I got it— "which is why our visions are stronger when we're wearing the talisman."

"Precisely." She nodded. "That pendant has been worn or carried by many generations of Lockwoods, dating all the way back to Caroline Elizabeth. It's the most powerful focusing object in our possession, which is why I wanted you to have it."

"Wow." Caitlyn touched the pendant, which was lying on the table where we'd dropped it. "I knew it was old, but not that old."

"The diary belonged to Caroline's great-grandnephew," Grandmother Lockwood went on, patting the old book. "And each generation of Seers since then has added his or her thoughts to it. Your father often carried it in his back pocket."

I stared at the diary, awed by what she'd just said. This ratty old book had been one of our father's prized possessions. Suddenly I felt a little choked up, almost as if I might cry.

"So my favorite pair of jeans is probably all charged up with vision power, too, huh?" I said to cover.

Grandmother Lockwood pursed her lips. "Please try to focus, Cassandra," she said. Then she pulled something else out of her purse—a tattered plaid wool scarf. "This belonged to your father as well."

She dropped the scarf on top of the diary and talisman. "We'll try it again with all three objects."

"Wait, I have a question." Caitlyn actually started to raise her hand as if she were at school. What a dork! "Are you trying to get us to have visions about each other? Me and Cass, I mean. Because we're not touching anybody else."

I hadn't thought about that. "Good point. Maybe we should try touching you," I told our grandmother. Two birds, one stone, right? Maybe if we got more visions about her, we'd learn something useful. After all, she didn't seem to be in any hurry to share.

But the old woman was shaking her head. "I forgot to mention that part," she said. "The theory behind focusing objects—"

"Hang on—theory?" I broke in. "So you don't really know if it's true?"

She ignored me. "The theory is that the power stored within focusing objects is for general Sight," she said. "When you touch another person, part of that person's own natural energy is what fuels and guides the details of the vision."

"Huh?" Caitlyn said, pretty much expressing my own reaction.

"Don't they teach any science in your American schools?" Grandmother Lockwood snapped. "It's a very simple principle. When you touch a specific person, you get a vision about that person. Yes?"

"Yes," we chorused.

"Mostly," Caitlyn added. "I mean, except for that vision about the guy with the braid when I was touching Cassie."

"Precisely." Grandmother Lockwood nodded. "The general energy from the diary fueled a random vision. Or seemingly random." She frowned slightly. "We're not quite sure how it works yet; your father was just beginning to formulate this theory when he . . . Well, never mind. We can test it now, hmm?"

I was still a little confused. "So you're saying if Cait and I touch that scarf that belonged to our father, whatever we see won't have anything to do with him, or with anyone we know, probably? It'll just add power to whatever vision we do end up having?"

She shrugged. "As I said, that's the theory."

"So what's the point?" I said. "Why do we even want to see some random person's future?"

"Yeah," Caitlyn added. "If we want to test our power with objects, we could use something of Mom's. Maybe we'd get a vision about her."

"I told you, it doesn't work that way." Grandmother Lockwood sounded awfully certain for a lady who'd just been talking about all this as a theory. "Ordinary objects don't add any power at all—only those that have been in a Lockwood's possession during a vision. John was fairly certain about that part."

"Fairly certain?" Caitlyn tilted her head.

Meanwhile I couldn't resist reaching for the scarf the old woman had dropped on the table. The wool felt scratchy and soft at the same time. "So this belonged to him, huh?" I murmured, talking mostly to myself.

"Yes." Grandmother Lockwood stood and grabbed the scarf. "Sit closer together—I want to try something."

Caitlyn scooted her chair up right next to mine. Then Grandmother Lockwood draped the scarf over both of our shoulders, tucking the ends down into the collars of our shirts.

"Keep the fabric as close to your heart as possible," she said. "We don't know if that makes a difference, but it's worth a try." She pushed the diary and necklace closer. "And touch these again, too."

I rolled my eyes. "Why bother?" I muttered, reaching for them. "Like I told you, you can't just—"

I gasped as the vision slammed into me. The familiar room faded almost to nothing, replaced by a bedroom I had never seen before, with elegant furnishings and plush carpeting. Even the messily unmade bed looked luxurious and soft. The single window I could see had thick iron bars on it, and pale moonlight was pouring in from outside. A thin, rather ragged-looking white man around my mother's age was standing near the door. He was dressed in a shabby velvet robe and slippers. Another man, this one at least ten years older and dressed in a dapper suit, was in the open doorway. Both men glanced around as they talked, seeming furtive and nervous. A second later the shabby man handed something to the other guy, though it was small enough that I couldn't see what it was. The dapper guy nodded, then spun on his heel and left the room, closing the door firmly behind him. The shabby man's shoulders slumped, and he started walking slowly toward the window . . .

"Oh!" Cait exclaimed.

The vision disappeared. My sister had fallen

back, losing contact with the diary and me. I gulped for breath, trying to bring the real world into focus.

"That was . . . intense," I managed to croak out.

"What did you see?" Grandmother Lockwood asked.

I glanced at Cait, who still looked out of it. "Two random guys in a room," I began.

"No," Caitlyn blurted out. "Not totally random. I—I recognized one of them."

"You did?" I blinked at her. "Which one?"

"The younger one." She sat up, carefully pulling off the scarf and setting it on the table. "It was the guy from my earlier vision—the one I saw with Mom."

My eyebrows shot up in surprise. "You mean her new Christmas boyfriend?" I exclaimed. "That shabby, tired guy—really? But he didn't look anything like our dad."

Caitlyn shrugged, picking up the talisman and fiddling with it restlessly. "He looked thinner and a little more tired than in the first vision, yeah. But I'm pretty sure it was the same guy."

I closed my eyes, trying to bring up the image of the shabby man's face. "Okay, I guess I can see it . . ."

Grandmother Lockwood hadn't said a word. When I opened my eyes and looked over, she was staring straight ahead, her expression distant and strange.

"So what does it mean?" I demanded. "I guess the visions aren't totally random after all."

"Yes, this is most interesting," she replied slowly, picking up the scarf and staring at it. "I'll have to discuss it with the others."

"What others?" I traded a look with my sister. "You mean other Lockwoods?"

Before she could answer, the front door slammed open and Mom stormed in. "Not cool, Verity!" she exclaimed.

Grandmother Lockwood swallowed hard, her expression returning to its haughty default. "Whatever are you on about, Deidre?"

Mom glared at her, arms akimbo. "You faked that text," she snapped. "Just admit it. Why are you so eager to get me out of your hair? No, never mind—I don't care why. But I'm getting fed up with it. If you want to have any contact with the girls at all, you need to respect my authority."

"Fine," Grandmother Lockwood retorted. "But only when you respect their unique heritage and stop trying to interfere with it!"

The argument continued from there, but I stopped paying attention. I'd just noticed that the scarf had disappeared. Grandmother Lockwood must have tucked it back in her purse when Mom came in. That was kind of weird, but I supposed she was worried that Mom might recognize it, if my dad had really worn it that much. Maybe she'd want to have it as a keepsake—not that Mom was the keepsake type.

I rubbed my fingers together, feeling a tiny piece of fiber that had come loose from the scarf. *This thread is the only thing I have of Dad's,* I thought, only half joking.

Did Grandmother Lockwood have more of his stuff? I wanted to ask her, but was afraid to do it with Mom there. Then again, maybe if I did she'd actually answer . . .

Before I could decide, Grandmother Lockwood grabbed the diary and stormed out, saying she'd be in touch when she could. As soon as she was gone, Mom rounded on us, still looking angry.

"There it is," I blurted out, realizing I was seeing yet another vision come true. At the pool party, I'd had a brief vision of Mom looking furious like this, with only the dingy white wall of the dining area in view behind her.

"What?" she snapped irritably. "Do you have something to say to me, Cassandra?"

"Nope." I glanced at Caitlyn. "We should get started on our homework," I added with a meaningful eyebrow waggle.

She nodded. "Right behind you."

Leaving Mom to cool off, we hurried to our room and shut the door. I flopped onto my bed and stared up at the ceiling.

"Well, that was interesting," I declared. Suddenly remembering something, I sat up again abruptly. "Wait—the talisman! Is it still out there with Mom, or did Granny L take it?"

"Neither." Cait opened her hand to show the

pendant nestled there. "I hid it in my lap when Mom came in."

"Good." I stared at her. "So you really think it was the same guy? In both those visions?"

She nodded. "I know it was. I just don't know what he was doing in this new vision. Who was the other man?"

"No clue." I leaned back against my pillows. "I still don't really understand why we're seeing random people now. I mean, at least the first time Mom was in the vision, too, right? So maybe that's the connection to Boyfriend Dude. But what about the vision from before—the guy with the braid and the camera? Who's he?"

"I don't know." She sat down at her desk. "I don't quite understand it either. I'm not even sure Grandmother Lockwood does."

"Great," I muttered. "The blind leading the blind." Then I thought of something else and sat up again. "Hey, but we had the same vision both times, right? So what's that about?"

"You mean how can what we saw be good and

bad at the same time?" Cait shrugged. "It's probably something like with the package from our grandmother."

I nodded. "It was good, because we finally found out she existed," I said. "But bad because Mom took it away. So what—does that mean you'll think Mom's new shabby boyfriend is super cool, and I'll think he's a dork?"

"He wasn't so shabby-looking in the other vision," she said with a little frown. "Anyway, I guess something like that is possible. Or maybe—maybe Mom will be happy with him at first, but he'll end up breaking her heart?"

I didn't like the sound of that. "Or that he's cool, but then he gets sick and that's why he looked all shabby?" Okay, I didn't like the sound of that either. "Whatever. Maybe we should stop worrying about it."

"But what if we're seeing these visions for a reason?" Caitlyn fretted. "Like we're supposed to stop something terrible, or—"

A sudden knock on the door made us both jump.

"Dinner's in the oven." Mom's voice was muffled but thankfully sounded calmer. "Come out here and set the table."

"Coming!" I called back, almost relieved to be interrupted. Because thinking about everything that had happened was making my brain hurt, and thinking about which side of the plate the forks go on was just about all I could handle right then.

10
CAITLYN

THE NEXT MORNING I wandered toward homeroom, lost in thought. Yesterday had been pretty crazy. I reached up to touch the talisman. It was pretty strange to think that seemingly ordinary objects could bring on such extraordinary visions. And also weird to imagine how many other Lockwoods had worn this very necklace over the past three hundred years.

But all of those thoughts disappeared as I stepped into homeroom and got a look at Liam. "Whoa," I said, hurrying forward. "What happened to you?"

He looked up at me with a grin. His face was painted bright green and orange, with crazy scales traced out in black, and yellowish fangs drawn sticking out of his mouth.

"Do you like it?" he asked. "I'm Viperguy—*rowr!*" He made claw hands at me.

Now I got it. Viperguy was one of his favorite comic book characters. He talked about him all the time. But why had he suddenly decided to go all cosplay about it—especially at school?

Bianca looked up from her book and rolled her eyes. "It was Goober's dare."

"Yeah, he dared me to let him and Josh paint me up as my favorite comic book character and then walk around like this all day." Liam sounded pretty cheerful about it.

"Yo, Liam!" Buzz rushed over. "Cool face paint, dude! Viperguy, right?"

"Yeah, thanks." Liam high-fived him. "It's for Truth or Dare."

Brent and Biff came over, too. As the three B

Boys admired Josh and Goober's handiwork, I sat down and glanced at the empty teacher's desk at the front of the room.

"Is Ms. X back today?" I asked Bianca.

She shrugged. "Haven't seen her yet."

I nodded, then glanced over at the boys. Biff was using a pen to touch up a smudged section of scales on Liam's chin. "Thanks, Biff," Liam said when he finished.

"No prob." Biff capped the pen and stuck it in his pocket. "Looking good, man!"

Liam's new friendship with the B Boys still seemed a little strange, even though I'd foreseen it in a vision. Of course, it hadn't seemed like that was what was happening at first. All I'd seen was Liam all bloody, with the B Boys dragging him along through the pool area at our birthday party. Cassie and I had been afraid that the football players were going to beat him up or something.

But as it turned out, the blood had been a result of Liam's own clumsiness. And the B Boys were just trying to help by carrying him over to a lounge chair.

Ever since that day, they'd all become pretty friendly.

Just goes to show how confusing our visions can be.

Suddenly Liam poked me in the arm. "Truth or dare," he said.

"What?" I blinked at him.

"Truth or dare." Liam sat back and grinned at me. "I know I'm technically not done with my dare until the end of the day. But I don't want to wait that long for my turn. So truth or dare, Cait."

Somehow I'd managed to avoid the game that had been sweeping the school. I had too many other things on my mind.

"Um, that's okay," I said. "You can pick someone else."

"No way, Waters!" Brent whooped. "My man Liam picked you, so you gotta take your turn!"

"Yeah," Biff and Buzz chorused.

Gabe Campbell wandered toward us, hands stuffed in the pockets of his jeans. "What are you losers yelling about over here?" he demanded.

"Liam just picked Caitlyn for Truth or Dare," Biff replied. "So what's it gonna be, Waters?"

"Yeah, Waters." Gabe stared at me, eyes glinting with malice. "What's it gonna be?"

I shivered, telling myself to be glad that it was Liam choosing me instead of Gabe. I could only imagine what kind of dare he might come up with. And I didn't want to think about what kind of truth question he would ask me!

"Okay, okay," I said quickly. "Uh, truth, I guess."

Liam looked disappointed. "Truth? Are you sure?"

I nodded. Truth definitely seemed quicker and easier to deal with. After all, I had no secrets from my friends—at least none that Liam would think to ask about.

"Okay," Liam said with a shrug. He thought for a second. "Here's your question. Why don't you ever want to talk about the class trip with me and Bianca?"

I gulped, realizing he had a point. The two of them had been discussing the upcoming trip practically every homeroom and lunch period all week. But I couldn't tell everyone the truth about why I didn't have much to say—namely, that I was way too distracted because my long-lost grandmother had just popped over from England, and my visions of the future were getting stronger and more frequent, and I was worried that something terrible might have happened to our homeroom teacher . . .

"Changed my mind," I blurted out. "A dare would be more fun, right?"

Liam's eyes lit up. "Awesome! I came up with some really good ones."

But Gabe pushed forward with a scowl. "No way!" he said, sounding kind of aggressive. "You can't change your pick."

"The rules don't say that, and besides, she's right. Dares are way more fun," Buzz said.

Everyone else nodded. Gabe muttered something about stupid games, and stomped away. Good. He'd always made me a little nervous, and now that Cass and I knew he'd run to Ms. Xavier with our secret, I liked him less than ever.

Speaking of Ms. Xavier . . . I glanced at the door, but there was no sign of either her or the sub from the day before. *That's a good sign,* I told myself. *Ms. X always comes in at the last second, and the sub got here earlier yesterday.*

I turned back to my friends. Liam was rubbing his hands together eagerly, like some evil scientist from a movie. Paired with the green and orange face paint, it was actually a little unnerving.

"Okay, lay it on me," I said with a weak smile.

"I've got the perfect dare for you," he said. "I dare you to put on a blindfold, then try to identify people by touching their faces."

Brent laughed. "Cool dare, bro!"

The others looked impressed, too. Biff dug a bandana out of his pocket.

"Here, you can use this as a blindfold," he said, tossing it to me.

I caught it, feeling trapped. The talisman felt cold and heavy against my skin. What if all that face-touching brought on a vision? With everyone looking at me, there would be no way of hiding it.

But what could I do? I'd already backed out of the truth question. No way could I get away with ditching this dare. I would just have to hope for the best.

Bianca helped me tie on the blindfold. Then I waited as Liam whispered with the others nearby. How long until the bell rang? Maybe we'd have to put this off until lunchtime. At least that way I'd be able to take off the talisman.

"Okay, here's your first face," Liam's voice said loudly in my ear, startling me. "Put your hands out."

I lifted both hands. Liam—at least I guessed it was him—grabbed them and guided them to a face. I felt around the nose and eyes, then moved up to the hair.

"Easy one," I said with a smile, realizing only one person I knew had hair that short. "Buzz."

"Yo, you got me!" Buzz's familiar voice exclaimed. "I should have put on a hat."

I waited for Liam to bring someone else forward. This time it took me a little longer to identify Maggie, a quiet kid who sat near the door who I finally recognized because of her funky hoop earrings. The next one was hard, too, but when Brent started snorting with laughter I knew it was him.

"Okay, I have the perfect person to go next," Liam said. "Ready, Cait?"

I nodded. This was actually kind of fun. It was amazing how different it was to use my sense of touch to identify someone instead of relying on sight. "Ready," I said.

The next face appeared beneath my fingers. I'd barely started feeling around the cheekbones when buzzing filled my head.

It was weird getting a vision with a blindfold on. There was no faded version of reality to distract me from the vivid scene I was experiencing.

The vision showed Lavender Adams being dragged by the wrist down a city sidewalk, looking annoyed. I couldn't see who was pulling her—he was just out of my line of sight—but the rest of the scene was super bright and clear, just as the visions always were when I was wearing the talisman. I could see a woman walking past and giving Lavender a curious look, a dog sniffing at a fire hydrant, and a big sign in English and Spanish advertising souvenirs and snacks.

"L-Lavender!" I managed to gasp out.

The face pulled back, and the vision was gone. I yanked down the blindfold and saw Lavender staring at me. The crowd watching had grown, too. At least half the class was gathered around my desk. Oh well, at least Gabe hadn't come back.

"Skip the drama, Caitlyn," Lavender said in her usual snotty way. "It's not like you're receiving messages from beyond to help you figure out who's who. At least in my case." She smiled and touched her face. "I mean, anyone could recognize me just from my super-high cheekbones."

"Yeah, you're right." I swallowed hard, trying to sound normal. "Anyway, can we stop now?"

"We still have time." Liam tugged the bandana back up over my eyes. "This is fun—let's at least do one more. Hold on . . ."

I sighed, waiting for my heartbeat to slow to normal. There were more muffled whispers, and then another face.

My shoulders tensed, but no vision came this time. Whew! I felt around the new face, trying to figure out who it might be. Biff? No, too small.

"Bianca?" I guessed.

"Guess again." Liam sounded pleased with himself.

I tried the names of a few other girls from my homeroom. But none of them were right. Finally the face cleared its throat.

"I think we'll have to wrap this up," it said. "It's almost time for the bell. It's me, Caitlyn. Miss Marin."

That was the substitute from yesterday. I pulled down the blindfold again and gave her a weak smile.

"Oh, hi," I said. "Um, I guess Ms. Xavier is still out sick or whatever?"

"Yes, I'm afraid you're stuck with me again." She chuckled, then clapped her hands. "Everyone to your own desks, people! Get ready for morning announcements."

I slumped down in my seat, my mind wandering back to the vision about Lavender. That definitely hadn't been Aura in the background. Was it San Antonio—maybe our class trip? If so, what was going on? Lavender had looked kind of upset . . .

"Pretty cool dare, huh?" Liam said.

"Not bad," Bianca agreed. "Very creative."

I nodded. "It was kind of fun."

Except for the creepy vision part, I added silently, trying not to shudder.

I could only hope that whatever happened to Lavender turned out to be a good thing in disguise, just like the vision of Liam at the pool. Otherwise, it could mean that our visions were changing again. What if all of Grandmother Lockwood's testing was messing things up? What if my good visions were getting mixed up with Cassie's bad ones?

Miss Marin was bending over some papers on Ms. Xavier's desk. I stared at her, feeling vaguely uneasy. It seemed awfully coincidental that the wacky teacher had disappeared immediately after my grandmother had learned about the whole social studies project fiasco.

But that's all it is, I told myself firmly. *A coincidence. Right?*

11

CASSIE

"WAIT, WAIT, I'VE got it!" Minion Abby giggled loudly. "Wait. No I don't . . ."

I winced, wondering if her laughter had always been so shrill. We were in homeroom, and Brayden had just dared Abby to peel a banana with her feet. Cute, right? Only not. I was already over the stupid game, but the rest of the school was still crazy for it. Emphasis on *crazy*. Some seventh grader had brought a live goat to school as her dare, and I'd heard there was an eighth grader who had been singing everything he said all day. One kid in our class had even dared another to climb the flagpole out front, though the principal had put a stop to that one.

"Use your other toe, Abs," Megan suggested, leaning forward for a better look.

Emily giggled. "Abby, you better not dare me to eat that banana when you're done with it."

"Ew!" several people chorused.

Brayden grinned. "Told you guys it's harder than it sounds."

"Yeah, good one," I told him, trying to get into the spirit of the game. "How'd you come up with a dare like that?"

He shrugged. "Brainstorm, I guess."

"Well, Abby's having fun with it, anyway."

"Yeah, I guess."

Just then the banana slipped out of Abby's grip and squirted off across the room. She chased it down, laughing loudly.

Brayden cleared his throat and shot me a sidelong look. "Actually, I only asked Abby 'cause she'd been hounding me all day to pick her next," he said quietly.

"I was thinking about asking someone else."

My breath caught in my throat. But I played it cool. "Oh yeah?" I said, all casual like. "Who?"

"Wouldn't you like to know?" He waggled his eyebrows and elbowed me.

I gasped as a vision swept over me. It was short, since Brayden's arm only touched mine for a second. Just an abrupt, blurry image of Brayden being helped up the steps of a bus . . . by Caitlyn.

"You okay?" Brayden looked concerned as I came out of it.

For a second I wished I could just tell him the truth—I wasn't okay, and everything definitely wasn't fine. Not even close.

But no, bad idea. There was no way he'd believe me. He'd just think I was crazy, like Gabe did.

"Guess I was all breathless thinking about who you might have almost picked for Truth or Dare," I said, going for flirty and playful.

I guess it worked, because he blushed a little and grinned. "I do have that effect on the ladies sometimes."

"I see." I fanned myself as if overcome, and he laughed.

Megan heard him and looked over. When she saw me and Brayden laughing together, she raised her eyebrows and then smiled at me approvingly.

Abby, on the other hand, had finally finished her dare and looked over just in time to see Brayden elbow me again—no vision this time, thank goodness—and she looked peeved.

"Hey!" she said, hurrying over with the banana. "I did it."

"Cool." Brayden smiled. "Guess it's your turn to pick someone."

Abby frowned slightly. "Fine." She narrowed her eyes at me. "Cassie—truth or dare?"

"Dare, I guess." What can I say? I'm daring. Besides, with everything going on, the truth seemed scarier than any possible dare right now.

At that moment our homeroom teacher strode in. "Seats, people," Mr. Bustamonte said. "Time for morning announcements."

"Oh well," I said. "We'll have to pick this up at lunch."

"Fine." Abby shrugged. "That'll give me time to think of something really good."

I slid into my seat behind Megan. The first announcement was about the class trip. "Be sure to sign up with your partner by Friday, or one will be assigned to you. The final list and bus assignments will go up next Wednesday morning," the school secretary said. "That's one week from today, y'all."

As the announcements continued, I leaned forward and tapped Megan on the shoulder. "Hey," I whispered. "Want to be partners?"

She shot me an apologetic look over her shoulder. "Sorry," she whispered back. "Lav already signed me up with her."

I sat back in my seat and glanced at Abby and Emily. I'd heard them talking about signing up together, so that was a no go, too.

Oh well. I wasn't too worried. There were a bunch of minor minions in the other section who I could ask. Or maybe someone else . . .

My gaze wandered toward Brayden, and I felt myself blushing. Yeah, right. He'd probably already signed up with one of the other B Boys. But whatever.

Finding a buddy for the class trip? Least of my problems right now.

I'D BARELY TAKEN three steps out of homeroom when Cait raced up to me. "Here," she hissed, shoving something into my hand. "I don't want to wear this anymore."

It was the talisman, of course. "We have to stop meeting this way," I joked.

"Whatever." She gave me a little push as she turned away.

And that second touch was the one that brought on a vision. It was brief, like the one about Brayden, but much more vivid. It showed Caitlyn hanging out with the Nerd Squad at Bianca's locker. They were looking over at another locker nearby—Emily's. A bunch of cards and stuff were taped to the outside, though I barely got a look at them before the vision winked out again.

"Urgh," I said as I came out of it.

Cait heard me and turned back. "What?"

I glanced around. Students were rushing past us

in every direction, heading to first period. I grabbed Caitlyn's arm and pulled her to a quiet spot by the water fountain. Grandmother Lockwood would probably have a stroke if she knew I was going to talk about the Sight in public, but oh well. This time I was sure Gabe Campbell wasn't anywhere within earshot.

"Vision," I whispered, and then jumped into what I'd seen. "Those had to be get-well cards. Which means something bad is going to happen to Emily." I sighed. "Just what we need on top of everything else, right?"

"Yeah." Cait bit her lip. "Speaking of which, Ms. Xavier's absent again today."

I shrugged. "Great. That's one more day she can't bug us about that stupid project."

"On my way out of class, I asked the sub if she knew what was wrong." Caitlyn tugged on her hair, looking worried. "She said she didn't know, but the school wanted her to be available to fill in indefinitely."

"Maybe Ms. X has the flu." I shrugged again.

Caitlyn frowned. "Aren't you the least bit worried that a certain someone we know might have something to do with it?"

"Oh, please." I snorted. "We have enough real drama going on without looking for more. Granny L had nothing to do with this."

"I don't know how you can be so—" Caitlyn cut herself off as Megan hurried over to us.

"Hi, Caitlyn," Megan said with a sunny smile. "Ready to head to math, Cass?"

"Sure." I shot my sister a look. "Right behind you."

12

CAITLYN

I KNEW MY sister wasn't worried about Ms. Xavier, but I was. I tried to talk to her about it again when I ran into her in the hall on the way to lunch, but her friend Abby caught up to us before I could say anything.

"Ready for your dare, Cassie?" she singsonged, ignoring me.

Cassie looked irritated for a split second, but then she shot Abby a sunny smile. "I was born ready," she said. "I just hope you're not going to make me cartwheel down the hall like that girl we saw on the way to third period."

"Or the poor kid she clonked on the head with her foot," Abby agreed with a laugh.

I hadn't heard about that. Then again, I'd been doing my best to ignore the whole Truth or Dare thing. Still, I couldn't help trailing along behind the two of them as they hurried into the cafeteria, a little curious in spite of myself. What would Abby ask my sister to do?

Liam and Bianca were just emerging from the lunch line. "Let's sit over here," I told them, waving toward a table near the one where Cassie and her friends usually sat. "My sister's about to do a dare, and I want to see."

"Sure." Liam set his tray down.

"What's she going to do?" Bianca asked.

"Not sure yet." I glanced over at Cassie's table as I sat. She and Abby were surrounded by Megan and Co., the B Boys, and various other popular kids. I couldn't hear what they were saying over the general din of the caf.

But a second later, Lavender looked our way and smirked. "Check it out, Cassie," she said loudly. "Looks like you've got an audience already."

Abby giggled. "Even better." She cleared her throat and raised her voice so everyone at the surrounding tables could hear. "Listen, everyone!" she announced. "You're invited to help with Cassie's dare, okay? She has to choose a popular song that everyone will know and act it out through, like, interpretive dance." She giggled again. "She can't stop until someone guesses the right song."

"Cool dare," Liam said with a snorty laugh. "Like Name that Tune without the tune."

Bianca laughed, but I didn't respond. Cassie had just turned and shot me a look, complete with eyebrow waggle. For a second I thought maybe she was embarrassed about performing her dare in front of the entire sixth grade.

But I got it when she stepped out to an open spot between tables and started to dance, flinging her arms around and snapping her head. I gasped as I flashed back to my vision—the one of her dancing in front of her silent friends in the cafeteria.

Sure enough, her friends were all watching intently. So was Liam. "Is it 'Dancing Queen'?" he called out.

That made the B Boys laugh, though Lavender just rolled her eyes. "Abs said it has to be a *popular* song, not a dorky one."

Cassie's other friends started shouting out the titles of recent pop hits. But I narrowed my eyes—there was something about the way Cass was making goggles around her eyes with her hands and then pointing at herself that stirred something in my memory.

"It's 'Look at Me' by Sakiko Star," I called out.

"Of course!" Lavender cried. "I don't know why I didn't get it right away."

Cassie collapsed into her seat, looking a little winded after her vigorous dancing. "I don't know why either," she complained. "And you call yourself a Sakiko fan?"

"No fair," Brent exclaimed. "Twins shouldn't be allowed to play. Don't you two have, like, ESPN or something?"

"ESPN?" Cass echoed, looking confused.

Megan laughed. "I think he means ESP."

As everyone started razzing Brent for his mistake, I lost interest and turned away. I definitely hadn't needed any twintuition to guess that song. Cassie only played it all the time—it was even the ringtone on her phone.

I pulled my sandwich out of my lunch bag. Liam and Bianca had already started talking about the math test we had coming up next period. That gave me a chance to think about Cassie's latest vision. Emily seemed to be turning up a lot in the visions lately, which made me wonder what was going to happen to her—and if we'd be able to figure it out in time to stop it this time.

Maybe Grandmother Lockwood would be able to help—if she showed up today, that was . . .

WHEN CASSIE AND I got home that afternoon, a familiar limo was parked at the curb. When we neared it, the driver's door swung open and Al hopped out.

"Good afternoon, twins," he greeted us cheerfully. "Your grandmother sent me to pick you up."

I was shocked. "Did our mother say it was okay?"

"Miz Lockwood figured you'd ask that." Driver Al whipped out a cell phone and handed it over.

Cassie peered over my shoulder as I scanned a text from Grandmother Lockwood. It said we were supposed to come back to the hotel for more testing, and that she'd called Mom at work to clear it with her.

"Sounds good," Cassie said. "I'm kind of surprised Granny L knows how to text, though. Score one for the older generation."

"Funny." I shot Al a smile, hoping he wouldn't tell Grandmother Lockwood that Cassie had said that. "Just let us dump our school stuff, and we'll be right back, okay?"

Moments later we were tooling along the highway toward Six Oaks. I was itching to talk about Ms. Xavier, or the Sight, or the Emily visions, or anything important at all, really, but Al was right there and he seemed to be in a chatty mood.

"How was school today, ladies?" he asked with a glance in the rearview.

"Fine," I said.

"Kind of fun, actually," Cassie added, getting pretty chatty herself. "There's this big game of Truth or Dare going around school . . ." She quickly filled him in on the basics.

"Sounds like something the kids would love and the teachers would hate," the driver said with a chuckle. "So have you two been picked yet?"

"Actually, I did a dare today," Cassie said. She filled him in on her dance dare. "I'm pretty sure Abby wanted to embarrass me by making me look goofy, but it was actually pretty fun."

"So did you get to pick someone after that?" Al asked. "That's how the game works, right?"

"Totally." Cassie grinned. "That was even more fun. I dared this guy Brent from the football team to change into girls' clothes and wear them for the rest of the lunch period."

Now that she mentioned it, I vaguely recalled noticing the tall B Boy wandering around the cafeteria wearing a skirt. But I'd had too much on my mind to worry about it at the time.

"Where'd he get the clothes?" I asked.

"Donations from all of us girls who were there," Cassie said. "Plus Biff ran and got some granny glasses from the lost and found. Brent looked awesome! He even let Megan put lip gloss on him." She grinned, then launched into describing every other dare she could think of, from Liam's Viperguy getup to the goat thing to some kid eating a whole bunch of hot peppers and ending up at the school nurse's office.

When we reached the hotel, our grandmother was waiting rather impatiently in her room. Actually, it was more of a suite, with a separate living room and kitchenette. There were fresh flowers in vases, plush carpet, and a marble-topped dining table—super fancy. Grandmother Lockwood looked pretty fancy herself in a black dress and tasteful gold jewelry.

"Sit down, girls," she said without bothering to say hello or ask about our day. "We might not have much time."

That seemed like an odd thing to say, but I sat at

the table with Cassie next to me. The marble table-top felt cool and hard under my elbows.

"What's the big hurry?" Cassie asked. "Do we have time to tell you about our latest visions?"

"Yes, of course." Grandmother Lockwood sat down across from us. "Tell me."

We filled her in on what we'd seen that day. She listened silently, nodding when Cassie told her how my cafeteria dance vision had come true.

"That's another one that seemed like it might be bad, but wasn't," I added. "I mean, when I had the vision I thought it was weird that all Cassie's friends were staring at her while she spazzed out—"

"You mean showed off my awesome moves," Cass corrected.

"Whatever." I laughed. "Anyway, it turned out to be fine."

"Yes, it's fascinating the way the visions break down between the two of you." Grandmother Lockwood got up and grabbed a shopping bag off a chair nearby. "But let's move on for now. I've got a few more focus objects here that belonged to your father, along with some other family heirlooms. I thought we'd try using several of them along with the talis-man and diary to see what happens."

I leaned forward, eager to see our dad's things—but also nervous. The visions we'd been getting during these tests were kind of creepy. I wasn't sure I wanted another one.

"Do you really think this stuff will help bring on more visions?" Cassie watched as Grandmother Lockwood took out a pair of wire-rimmed glasses, a battered wallet, some old coins, and a single leather glove.

"That's the theory." Grandmother Lockwood pulled an old-fashioned and slightly moth-eaten ladies' hat out of the bag and set it with the other stuff. Finally she added the diary and scarf to the pile. "Stacking the talismans means adding more stored power. We'll have to see if that changes things."

"Changes things how?" I asked.

"Like bringing on the visions when you wish to have them," she replied. "And perhaps helping you focus, making things clearer and easier to understand." She pushed the little tower of objects toward us. "Based on what happened yesterday, I consider it a good working theory."

"Whatever." Cassie grabbed the glasses and studied them. "I'm up for anything that might give us some control over when we have visions. Because it's really pretty embarrassing when I—"

"Hold that thought," Grandmother Lockwood said as the buzz of a cell phone rang out from her purse.

She hurried over and answered. I glanced at my sister, still anxious about what we were doing.

I forgot about that when I heard the squawk of a loud voice coming out of the phone. Uh-oh.

"Is that Mom?" Cass murmured. "She doesn't sound happy."

"Settle down, Deidre," Grandmother Lockwood said into the phone. "I didn't kidnap anyone. I left you a message—perhaps you didn't get it?"

More squawking from Mom. I felt light-headed for a second, not sure why the whole scene was weirding me out all of a sudden. Okay, I did know one reason—it sounded as if our grandmother hadn't actually cleared this visit with Mom after all, which was bad news. But it was more than that . . .

Then my mind cleared as I got it. "This was my vision," I whispered to Cass. "The one of Grandmother Lockwood on the phone."

She lifted her finger to her lips. She was listening to the argument going on across the room. We couldn't really hear what Mom was saying, though we could certainly imagine it.

Grandmother Lockwood sighed loudly. "Let's not punish the girls for a misunderstanding between you and me," she said. "They only came because I told them you said it was all right. And it's important that I see them while I can. Things may be much more urgent now, remember?"

Cassie and I traded a confused look. What did that mean? Was she talking about the way the visions were getting stronger and more frequent?

"Girls," Grandmother Lockwood said, holding her phone out to us. "Your mother would like to speak with you."

Cassie grabbed the phone, holding it out a little ways from her ear so I could press in and hear. "Mom?" she said. "It's us."

"Sorry, we thought you okayed this," I added.

"It's all right," Mom said, though she still sounded pretty cranky. "You haven't known your grandmother for very long; you don't know how she can— Well, never mind."

Grandmother Lockwood was watching us from across the table, her arms folded over her chest. Had she pushed Mom too far this time? I was expecting Mom to order us to come home right this minute.

"What do you want to do?" Mom asked instead. "Would you like to stay there? If not, I can come pick you up."

"No, it's fine, Mom," Cassie said. "We want to stay."

"If it's okay with you," I added despite an eye roll from Cass.

"Fine." Mom didn't sound particularly surprised. Fortunately, she didn't sound all that mad anymore either. Just kind of tired. "Be home in time for dinner, all right? And promise me you'll check in with me before going anywhere from now on."

"Yes, ma'am," I said.

"Sure thing," Cassie added.

We said good-bye and handed back the phone. Grandmother Lockwood spoke to Mom again briefly, then hung up.

"All right, that's settled." She rubbed her hands together and returned to her seat. "Let's get started."

She told us to join hands and also touch all of the objects at the same time. I obeyed gingerly, half expecting to be knocked out by some lightning bolt of a vision brought on by all that Lockwood stuff.

But nothing happened.

"Well?" Grandmother Lockwood said.

Cassie shook her head. "Nada," she said. "Guess it's not working this time."

"Hmm." Our grandmother frowned. "All right, let's try something else. Think back to that last vision—the one you had about the two men."

I didn't like the sound of that. Why did she want us to basically spy on total strangers? Wouldn't it make more sense to try to get a vision about someone we knew? There wasn't much point in predicting what those two men might do next, or the next time the guy with the long braid went Dumpster diving . . .

Suddenly my head filled with buzzing, and I was slammed into another vivid vision. I was looking at those trash cans again—the same ones Braid Guy had been digging through before. But this time he was nowhere in sight. Instead, a slender young woman was standing there, pointing at something in the can and yelling angrily. At least I guessed she was yelling, since all I could hear, as usual, was the loud buzzing. The young woman had sleek black hair pulled back in a ponytail, and was wearing sweatpants and a T-shirt. An oatmealy-looking facial mask covered her face, making it hard to tell what she looked like.

The vision didn't last long, since Cassie pulled her hand away a moment later, breaking us out of it. "Well?" Grandmother Lockwood asked.

"I didn't see those men," I told her. "But I'm pretty sure I saw the same place from the first stranger vision . . ." I went on to describe what I'd seen as best I could.

"Weird," Cassie said when I finished. "I didn't see anything like that at all."

"Really?" I was startled. "What did you see?"

"An old dude in a grungy-looking bathrobe," she said.

Grandmother Lockwood leaned forward. "Was it one of the men from the last vision?"

"Nope. This guy was way older than them—probably like seventy at least," Cassie said. "And actually, his robe was all dirty and gross, but it looked like it was real silk."

Leave it to fashion-crazy Cassie to notice a detail like that! "Where was the guy?" I asked.

"He was sitting in this huge dining room with, like, gold candlesticks and a white tablecloth and stuff," she said. "There was even a nice place setting. But he was using his fancy fork to eat sardines straight out of the can!" She made a face. "Wretched, right?"

"Sardines?" Grandmother Lockwood sounded

perplexed. "I don't understand."

"Me neither," Cassie said with feeling. "Sardines are totally gross!"

Our grandmother hardly seemed to hear her. She was staring into space. "I wish I had more resources here," she muttered. "This isn't making sense. Not unless . . ." She cut herself off and stood abruptly. "We should probably get you home so Deidre doesn't have a fit."

It seemed a little late for that, but I nodded. "This is the first time Cass and I had a vision together that didn't show the same thing," I said. "What does that mean?"

"I don't know." Grandmother Lockwood looked troubled. "The visions don't normally work that way. Then again, we've never had twin Seers before, so this is all new territory."

"That's us, new and improved," Cassie joked. "Hey, maybe we should consult with Ms. Xavier about it. She's an expert at all this weirdo stuff—or at least she thinks she is."

Our grandmother frowned. "That won't be

necessary," she said icily. "I've dealt with that lit-tle . . . problem."

Yikes! "What do you think she meant by that?" I whispered as she swept off into the bedroom.

Cassie shrugged, though she looked a bit wor-ried. "Who knows?" she said. "Maybe she found someone with the flu to cough in Ms. X's coffee."

We had to stop talking then as Grandmother Lockwood returned with her purse and jacket. "Let's go, girls," she said.

I was itching to discuss what had just happened with Cassie. But I was going to have to wait, since Grandmother Lockwood ended up riding back to Aura with us. Not that we could have talked freely in front of Al anyway.

It was a quiet ride home. Grandmother Lock-wood stared out the window without saying much. Cassie played with her phone. Even Al was pretty subdued aside from some humming.

Finally we pulled up in front of our house. "Come," Grandmother Lockwood said. "I need to speak with your mother."

The three of us climbed out. Cassie and I headed

for the front door, but our grandmother called us back.

"Give us a hug," she ordered. "I might not see you for a while."

"What?" I said, surprised. "Why not?"

Grandmother Lockwood pulled Cassie into an embrace and I blinked, recognizing yet another vision coming true in front of me. It had been such a minor vision that I'd nearly forgotten about it.

She reached for me next, and I hugged her, breathing in the light scent of jasmine and mothballs. "Are you going somewhere?" I asked.

"Yes, I might have to go away for a bit," she said. "But don't fret, I'll be back before long."

"But what if something happens, or we have questions, or . . . ," I began.

Grandmother Lockwood pulled two small pieces of paper out of her purse. "Here's an email address where I can be reached," she said, handing one scrap of paper to each of us. "It's only for emergencies, though, all right?"

I stared at the email addy, feeling dismayed. Just when we were starting to get somewhere! I mean,

I wasn't thrilled about the odd stranger visions. And Grandmother Lockwood didn't seem quite as knowledgeable about all the details of the Sight as I'd hoped. Still, she seemed to be our best bet for getting things under control.

Before I could say any of that, Mom hurried outside. "Go inside," she told us. "I was about to start dinner. Pasta's in the bag on the table."

"But—" Cassie began.

"Go!" Mom pointed.

What choice did we have? We went, leaving the two of them out in the yard together.

13
CASSIE

BY THE TIME I walked into social studies class on Thursday, people were starting to buzz about why Ms. Xavier had been out all week. Emily joked that she'd probably joined a cult, while Brayden and Megan speculated about alien abduction.

Me? I was trying not to think about it. I'd thought Caitlyn was crazy to think Grandmother Lockwood could have anything to do with our teacher's absence. But after yesterday, I wasn't so sure.

Brayden leaned across the aisle as Miss Marin

started passing back our quizzes from the day before. "Hey, did you hear?" he asked with a grin. "Brent came up with this awesome dare for Emily."

"Really?" I tried to focus on what he was saying. Looking at his adorable face made that a little easier. "What's the dare?"

"You know how she's always bragging about how fast she picked up snowboarding when her family went to Colorado last year?"

I shrugged. "No," I said. "I wasn't here last year."

"Oh, right." He blinked. "Wow. It's kind of hard to believe you've only been in Aura for like a month or two. I already can't even imagine this place without you."

He suddenly looked weirdly shy. Was he blushing? He leaned over, fiddling with his cast so his hair fell forward, hiding his face.

"Yeah, um, it feels like longer to me, too," I said, feeling awkward—but kind of psyched, too.

"Anyway." He sat up and cleared his throat. "So Ems went skiing with her family and kept sending everyone photos of herself on the slopes. She met this guy who taught her to snowboard, and she couldn't stop bragging about what a natural she was."

"Sounds annoying," I said, glancing forward at Emily two seats ahead.

He shrugged. "I guess, but Brent came up with a way to finally make her prove it."

"How?" Unless we had a sudden freak blizzard or something, I didn't get it. But I couldn't help flashing back to the vision of Emily and the ambulance. Could it be connected to this dare?

Brayden grinned playfully. "I swore I wouldn't tell," he said, his brown eyes twinkling. "Brent wants Emily to be surprised. Sorry. You'll have to wait and see. Just keep your fingers crossed that she chooses dare when he asks her."

I still felt uneasy. If something bad was going to happen to Emily, I needed to prevent it if I could. Otherwise, what was even the point of the stupid visions?

"Oh, come on," I wheedled, trying to sound flirty rather than desperate. "You can tell me. I won't breathe a word."

"Sorry, no can do." He crossed his heart with one finger. "I can't go back on my word to a bro."

"Sure you can." I tilted my head and gave him my best smile. "You might as well give in now. I always get what I want in the end."

"Oh yeah?" He grinned.

"All right, kids," Miss Marin said, dropping the last paper on someone's desk. "Hush up and let's get started."

Brayden shrugged, still grinning, and mouthed the word *sorry* at me.

I smiled weakly and slumped in my seat, feeling anxious and a little annoyed. Whatever Brent had in mind for Emily, it looked like this was one thing I wouldn't see until it happened.

"WHAT IF SHE never comes back?" Caitlyn said, wandering toward my desk.

I looked up from my homework. We were in our room waiting for Mom to get back with the takeout Mexican food she'd ordered. Being Aura, there was no delivery, so she'd had to go pick it up.

"You mean Granny L?" I said. "She'll be back."

"How do you know?" Caitlyn twisted her hair between her fingers, looking anxious. "I mean, she finally started telling us some stuff about the Sight. But there's so much more to know, and we can't do it on our own. I mean, we can try like we were before, but it's not like we were getting very far, and if Gabe tells anyone else or we make some dumb mistake, who knows what could happen or . . ."

Uh-oh. When Caitlyn gets going like that, she can talk for hours without really saying anything. "Chill," I said. "Seriously. It'll be all right."

I reached over and grabbed her hand. As soon as I touched it, I gasped as a vision came.

The Caitlyn standing in front of me faded away, and instead I saw a brighter, more vivid Caitlyn. She was standing in a brilliantly lit shop with posters of retro-looking women on the walls sporting all kinds of crazy hair colors—bright blue, purple, hot pink. Lavender was there, too. She was standing in a doorway, frowning. She said something—not that I could hear it, what with all the usual buzzing—and angrily tossed the magazine she was holding at Cait.

Cait yanked her hand away, breaking the vision. "What?" she demanded. "Did you see something about me?"

"Yeah." I took a few deep breaths, trying to get my racing heartbeat under control. "Don't worry, it was nothing scary. Just Lav being bratty."

"Well, that could be any day."

I told her what I'd seen. She looked confused. "Posters of purple hair? Where's that?"

"Got me." I shrugged. "I haven't been to Lav's house yet; maybe she has really weird taste in home decor."

"But why would I be at Lavender's house?" Caitlyn said. "We're not friends."

Just then we heard Mom holler from the front of the house. I pushed my homework away and stood.

"Come on," I said. "Whatever you did to annoy Lav, I doubt it's life or death. Let's worry about the important visions first, okay? But before that, let's eat. I'm starving."

14
CAITLYN

I DIDN'T SLEEP very well that night, and for once I couldn't blame it on Cassie's snoring. Every time I dropped off I had weird dreams—one was about Grandmother Lockwood talking to a bunch of ghosts with voices that sounded like buzzing, another featured a voodoo witch doctor doing weird experiments on Ms. Xavier and Emily, and in yet another the only thing I could remember was hanging on to a long, black braid to avoid falling into a deep pit. Creepy!

In the morning, I got dressed and dragged myself out to the kitchen for breakfast. Cassie and Mom were already there. Cass was playing with her phone and nibbling on some toast, while Mom was totally focused on her oatmeal and coffee.

"Cereal's on the counter," Mom told me when I came in.

I nodded and poured some into a bowl. After setting it down at my place, I reached for the milk.

It wasn't until the buzzing started that I realized Mom had been doing the same thing. Touching her hand had set off a vision.

Real Mom faded out, and Vision Mom took over, more vivid than any of my dreams. She was shaking and crying as she stared at something small and shiny in her hand. Aunt Cheryl was there, too, her arm around Mom's shoulders and a concerned and freaked-out expression on her face.

"Caitlyn?" Mom drew back, and the vision was gone. "Are you all right?"

Cassie looked up quickly. "What happened?"

Mom was staring at me. "I've seen that look

before," she said. "You had one of those—those visions?"

I gulped, shooting an anxious look at Cassie. Between my fuzziness from lack of sleep and the usual effects of the vision, it was harder than ever to recover and say something coherent. "I—um . . . ," I mumbled, not wanting to tell Mom what I'd seen. Not until I figured out what it meant anyway.

Maybe Cassie read something on my face, or maybe it was the old twintuition kicking in again. But she suddenly moved her elbow, knocking over her glass of orange juice.

"Oops!" she exclaimed, jumping to her feet.

"Cassie!" Mom got up, too, rushing over and doing her best to mop up the juice before it dripped on the floor. "How many times have I told you not to leave your glass right on the edge of the table?"

"Sorry." Cass caught my eye, trying to see if I was okay, before helping Mom wipe up the juice.

I gave her a shaky smile in return. Then I tried to get my mind back in gear.

By the time the O.J. was cleaned up and Mom

remembered to ask again about the vision, I was ready. "Yeah, I saw something," I told her. "I saw you smiling because Cassie showed you a good grade on a quiz."

"Oh." Mom nodded. "Sort of like that other time you told me about."

"Uh, yeah." I tried not to feel too guilty about lying. It was for her own good, after all. My visions were only supposed to show good stuff, right? So why worry her for no reason? For all I knew that shiny thing would turn out to be a winning lottery ticket or something. Not that it had looked anything like a lottery ticket . . .

"Hurry and finish eating," Cassie told me, shoving the last bite of her toast in her mouth. "We don't want to be late."

I pushed my bowl away. "I'm actually not that hungry. I think I'll just grab a granola bar and eat it as we walk."

Five minutes later, we were on our way and I'd just finished telling Cassie what I'd really seen. "Weird," she said. "I wonder what she was looking at."

"Yeah. And why Aunt Cheryl was there." I

thought back, trying to picture the background. "Actually, I think they might have been at Aunt Cheryl's house. I think I saw that striped wallpaper from her front hallway."

"Has Mom mentioned going to see Aunt Cheryl anytime soon?"

"Not that I've heard." I shrugged. "But who knows."

"So what did the thing look like?" Cassie asked. "All you said was that it's shiny. You mean shiny like a flashlight? Or like jewelry?"

"More like jewelry, I think. I couldn't see it that well."

"What kind of jewelry would make her freak out like that?" Cassie wondered. Then she shrugged. "Anyway, I don't blame you for not wanting to tell her. Mom's already a little sensitive about this whole Sight thing."

"Yeah." I still felt weird about lying, but it was too late to do much about it now. "Let's talk about something else. Have you figured out what's up with Emily?"

"Not really." Cassie chewed her lower lip. "I told

you what Brayden said about that dare, right? I guess Brent is going to give it to her today. I'll try to find out what it is, just in case."

We talked about that and Grandmother Lockwood until we got to school. Then Cassie gave me a wave and headed off toward her locker. I didn't need anything from mine that day, so I headed straight toward the first-floor hallway where Bianca's locker was. A couple of Cassie's friends had lockers there, too, and it was kind of the unofficial before-school meeting place for the whole popular crowd. At least usually it was—today there was no sign of them. But I didn't worry about it. For all I knew, they'd decided to start meeting up at someone else's locker instead.

Liam and Bianca were already in their usual spot, though. Liam was leaning against the wall, talking a mile a minute while Bianca dug around for her books. When I got closer, I could hear that they were talking about the class trip.

"I heard we'll have a couple of hours free afterward to do whatever we want," Liam was saying eagerly. "I was thinking we could go to the River Walk, or maybe the World's Fair thingy or—"

"Hi, guys," I broke in. "Wow, I can't believe the class trip is less than a week away."

"I can't wait," Liam said. Bianca closed her locker and the three of us started walking to homeroom. "The only part I'm not looking forward to is getting up extra early to make that six a.m. bus!" He snorted with laughter.

Bianca smiled. "It should be fun," she agreed. "I've never been to the Alamo."

My eyes widened. "Seriously?" I exclaimed. "But it's so close! You'll love it, though, it's amazing. By the way, are we still all going to sign up as trip buddies together?"

Liam blinked at me, then glanced at Bianca. "Oh," he said, looking uncomfortable. "The two of us already signed up as partners."

"You did?"

"Yeah." Bianca stopped just outside homeroom and gazed at me worriedly. "Sorry, Cait. We just assumed you were planning to be partners with

Cassie or something, since you never wanted to talk about it with us."

"Oh." I bit my lip. "I guess I've been sort of distracted lately. Sorry about that."

"It's okay," Liam assured me. "Maybe we can figure something out."

"No, it's no biggie." That distracted feeling was already coming back as I glanced inside and saw Miss Marin at Ms. Xavier's desk. Again. "Um, I'll probably just sign up with Cassie anyway."

"You sure?" Liam still looked concerned.

"Yeah. Come on, let's get inside before the bell rings." I hurried in, trying not to worry about what had happened to Ms. Xavier.

15

CASSIE

MY FRIENDS WEREN'T at Megan and Emily's lockers when I got there. I headed to homeroom, but none of them were there either.

I thought that was a little odd, but I actually didn't mind too much. I wasn't in the mood for random chitchat. That vision of Caitlyn's was bugging me, but I couldn't quite figure out why.

I leaned back in my seat, staring into space. Mom and Aunt Cheryl were sisters, and they'd always been close. So it wasn't a huge shock that Mom might visit sometime soon. But why would she be crying? And why would Aunt Cheryl look all shocked about it? And what was that little shiny thing?

Suddenly I sat up straight. "Little shiny thing," I murmured, flashing back to another little shiny thing I'd seen—in that vision about the dude with the braid. He'd pulled something small out of the trash can.

"Random," I muttered, slumping down again. Talk about a stretch. There were a lot of little shiny things in the world. And we didn't even know who that braid guy was. Why assume he had anything to do with Mom?

Then again, why not? It wasn't like we had a lot of other theories to work with, and almost all of our visions—except for Braidy and the two other dudes—had been connected to people we knew. There had to be a reason we were seeing those guys.

I snapped out of my thoughts as Mr. Bustamonte hurried into the room. He looked around and frowned. "Where is everybody?" he said.

I glanced around, too. Only about half the kids were there.

Before I could try to figure that out, everyone suddenly rushed in. "Sorry, Mr. B!" Emily cried, looking pink-cheeked and excited. "We're here!"

"Just in time," he said as the bell rang. "Sit down and be quiet for morning announcements."

Megan glanced back as she slid into her seat in front of me. "You missed it," she whispered with a giggle.

"Missed what?" I whispered back. But just then Mr. Bustamonte walked past our desks, clearing his throat, and we had to shut up. Megan mouthed the words *Tell you later* at me, then turned around.

The announcements took forever. By the time they finished, we had to book for first period. As we hurried down the hall, Emily elbowed me. "Did Megs tell you about my dare?" she asked with a giggle.

"Not yet." I looked over at Megan, suddenly remembering yet another worry from my long list. Had the dare already happened, and I'd missed it? If so, Emily still seemed to be in one piece. Good; maybe that was one thing I didn't have to worry about. "Is this the thing with Brent?" I asked.

Suddenly Caitlyn appeared, yanking me away

from my friends. "Hey!" I said.

"She's still out," Caitlyn hissed in my ear.

I gulped. "You mean Ms. X?" My friends had paused to wait for me, but I waved them on. "I'll catch up in a sec!" I called.

Caitlyn looked panicky as we ducked into a quiet corner. "Miss Marin was there for homeroom *again*," she told me. "Liam asked her if Ms. Xavier would be back in time to chaperone the class trip next week, but she said the principal already asked if she could go on the trip in Ms. X's place."

"Whoa." That couldn't be good. The trip wasn't until next Thursday. What kind of horrible illness could the teacher have that would last that long? "But you can't still think Granny L had something to do with it." Actually, I was kind of thinking that myself at this point, but I didn't want to believe it.

"You heard what she said yesterday." Caitlyn started chewing on her thumbnail. "She said she'd dealt with her. What if she did something horrible?" She swallowed hard and met my eye. "Like what I saw in that vision?"

I hated seeing my sister look so freaked out, so I shook my head, ignoring my own feelings that Caitlyn could be right. "Doubtful," I assured her. "Remember, you only see good stuff."

"What could possibly be good about lying unconscious—or maybe worse!—in a room full of skulls?"

"I don't know. But I know it definitely won't be good if I'm late for first period." I squeezed her hand. "Don't worry. We'll figure out what to do."

She smiled weakly, looking slightly less terrified. As we rushed off to our respective classes, I could only hope I was right.

ALL OUR TEACHERS knew that the entire sixth grade would have two days off from schoolwork the following week. The class trip was on Thursday, and then Friday was an in-service day so we didn't have to come to school. To make up for it, most of the teachers seemed to be cramming as much work as possible into the next few days. I barely had time to breathe that morning, let alone worry about Ms.

Xavier, Grandmother Lockwood, and the rest.

Finally the bell rang for lunch. "Ready for this?" Megan asked, sounding oddly excited. Then again, she does love fish stick Fridays in the caf.

"I'll meet up with you in a sec." I shoved my books in my bag. "I need to stop off at the library first."

"Okay, we'll try to wait for you." Megan giggled. "No promises, though!"

She rushed off with the Minions. I stared after them, confused. What had that been about?

But I didn't think about it for long. I had more important things to worry about. That little talk with Cait after homeroom had made me decide that enough was enough. I was tired of feeling worried and helpless. Especially the second part—worry is one thing, but I don't do helpless. Grandmother Lockwood didn't want to answer any of our questions? Well, it was time to *make* her answer at least some of them. And I'd finally figured out how to do it.

As I stepped out of the classroom, Brayden rushed past me. I flashed him a smile, but he didn't even seem to notice me standing there. He was shouting and waving at the other B Boys, who were a short distance down the hall. Brent lifted a skateboard over his head, grinned, and shot Brayden a thumbs-up.

It was just like Brent to suddenly decide to skateboard to class instead of walk. Principal Zale would love it.

Turning the opposite way, I hurried toward the library. Moments later I was logging on to my email account at one of the school computers. I dug into my pocket for that little scrap of paper Grandmother Lockwood had given me, with her email address written on it.

"What are you doing here?"

I looked up. Caitlyn was standing there blinking at me. "I could ask you the same thing," I said. "I thought you'd be first in line for fish sticks."

"Funny." She set her bag on the floor by the next computer. "I can't stop thinking about that Ms. Xavier vision. Or the one about Mom and Aunt Cheryl, for that matter." She shrugged. "I thought I might do a little research, see if I can find anything that might help us figure things out."

"I had a better idea to figure things out."

"What?" Cait glanced at the screen. "Checking email? Brilliant plan."

"Just wait." Closing my eyes, I thought about what to say. Then I opened up and started to type.

> Dear Grandmother, we know you're still keeping secrets
> from us. For instance, we know you did something
> to Ms. Xavier. You have to tell us what's going on.
> Otherwise we will be forced to tell Mom what you said.
> She's a police officer, you know, and she won't be able
> to ignore a possible crime.

"Are you kidding?" Cait was reading over my shoulder. "You can't write that. Way too aggressive."

Was she right? My finger hovered over the backspace button on the keyboard, but then I shook my head.

"I disagree," I said. I couldn't help noticing that she hadn't objected to my idea to email Granny L. Just my phrasing. "We need to write something she can't ignore. That's the only way we might get her to answer some of our questions. Anyway, what's the worst that could happen?"

I quickly signed the email from me and Caitlyn, then hit send before Cait could object.

She didn't. She just stood there chewing her lower lip. "Okay," she said at last. "I guess we'll see what happens."

"Yeah." I slung my bag over my shoulder. "Come on, let's go get some fish sticks."

When we stepped out of the library, I heard laughter from the direction of the west stairwell at the far end of the hall. I glanced that way and saw a bunch of people clustered at the bottom of the steps, staring and pointing up toward the second-floor landing.

Caitlyn noticed, too. "What's going on over there?"

"I don't know," I said. "And I'm way too hungry to care."

"Okay." Caitlyn turned toward the cafeteria. "It's probably just the B Boys goofing off. Brent almost crashed into me on his skateboard on my way to the library." She shook her head, going all prissy. "He's just lucky Principal Zale wasn't around."

I barely heard the last part. I gasped as everything suddenly fell into place in my mind. "Emily!" I blurted out. "Skateboard—oh, no!"

"Huh?"

"Emily's dare hasn't happened yet after all." I felt frozen in place as it hit me. "I never heard what Brent decided to make her do, but I'm pretty sure I just figured it out."

"Emily's dare?" Caitlyn sounded confused. "Is this about your vision?"

"You bet." I took off down the hall. "And it's about to play out—at least if we don't get there in time to stop it."

"But—" Cait began.

There was no time to explain further. "Stop!" I hollered as I sprinted toward the stairwell. "Wait!"

Halfway there, Principal Zale stepped out in front of me. "Whoa, young ladies," he said, holding up his hands. "No running in the halls."

Somehow I managed to skid to a stop before I crashed into him. But I danced to the side, itching to run again. "I have to go," I told him urgently, gesturing toward the stairs. "They're about to do something really stupid."

Down the hall, I could hear kids starting to chant "Go! Go! Go!"

By then Caitlyn had caught up. "Sorry, sir," she said breathlessly. "We just need to get over there."

I closed my eyes briefly, shuddering at the images that flashed through my mind. It didn't take the Sight to figure out what happened next.

"You've got to stop them," I blurted out, pointing. "That way. I'm afraid they'll get hurt—bad."

I tried not to think about what my friends would say if they found out I'd tattled. But I could worry about that later. Whatever was going to happen, it didn't look good for Emily. Not if people were going to end up decorating her desk with ribbons and her locker with cards. Not if she was going to be carried off on a stretcher.

Principal Zale looked doubtful for a second, but I guess something in my face told him this was for real. He took off down the hall, and Cait and I followed.

"What's going to happen?" she panted in my ear.

"Nothing, I hope." I crossed my fingers as I ran.

"Stop right there!" the principal bellowed, pointing up into the stairwell.

When we caught up, Emily was at the top of the steps, one foot on Brent's skateboard and a surprised look on her face. More people were crammed into the stairwell—lots more. It looked like almost half the sixth grade had turned out to watch Emily's dare. Talk about being the last to know. Well, second last. Obviously, Caitlyn and her dorky friends hadn't heard either.

"Aw, man!" Biff muttered.

But the principal was already charging up the steps. "Sorry, Principal Z," Emily said with an uncertain giggle. "We were just messing around."

"Yeah, dude," Brent added. "She has to do her dare."

"She'll be fine," Abby added. "She's a totally expert snowboarder. This is almost the same thing, right?"

"That's the dare," I murmured to Cait, who looked a little confused. "Brent dared Ems to show off her snowboarding skills by riding his board down the steps."

"Yikes," Cait said with a shudder.

I nodded, guessing she was thinking about our visions. I know I was.

Meanwhile Principal Zale was scowling around at everyone. "I knew this Truth or Dare craze would be trouble when I had to drag that young man off the flagpole the other day," he said. "From this moment on, the game is over, do you hear me? The next person I catch playing this game on school property gets a full week's suspension. And no class trip either."

There were groans and protests from all sides, but I slumped against the wall, relieved. I perked up when Brayden sidled toward me, keeping an eye on the principal, who was still ranting.

"Hey," Brayden said. "I was wondering if you were going to show up."

Caitlyn looked from me to Brayden and back again. "Excuse me," she said with a stifled giggle. "I need to, um . . ."

She scurried off. Subtle, Cait. Real subtle.

Luckily Brayden didn't seem to notice her goofy behavior. "Bummer about the game, huh?" he said.

"Yeah, I guess." I shrugged, trying to seem casual. "It was getting a little old anyway if you ask me."

"Too bad, because actually I had one more dare for you, if you're up for it."

"But it's not your turn," I reminded him.

"I guess I'm just a rebel," he joked. Then he cleared his throat. "So do you want to hear it?"

I couldn't imagine what he was about to say. But suddenly I really, really wanted to know.

"Yeah, I'm game," I said. "Lay it on me."

"I dare you . . . to be my partner for the class trip." He grinned, but he looked nervous. "What do you say?"

I was so surprised that I just burbled for a second. That so wasn't what I was expecting!

"Um, yes!" I blurted out at last. "I mean, sure. Sounds good." I shot him a sidelong smile. "Cool."

"Yeah, cool." He smiled back, looking relieved.

Then we had to step aside as Principal Zale swept past, dragging Emily with one hand and Brent with the other. Apparently it hadn't taken him long to get to the bottom of things.

I sent Emily a mental apology, though mostly I was just happy that she was okay. Once again, the visions had come through. Just barely.

"Get to lunch, the rest of you!" Principal Zale called over his shoulder as he headed for the office. "Now."

"You heard the man." Brayden poked me on the arm, which thankfully didn't bring on a vision. "Walk you to the caf?"

"Sure." I fell into step beside him, glad that at least there was one silver lining to this crazy, ridiculous, confusing week.

16
CAITLYN

"SO WHAT ARE the odds that Ms. Xavier will turn up at the game?" I said.

It was Saturday, and Cassie and I were getting ready to head over to the football game. Just about everybody in town went to the home games, including the teachers. In fact, we'd ended up sitting with Ms. Xavier at our very first Aura Middle School game.

Cassie looked up from pulling on a pair of socks and frowned. "I can't believe Granny L hasn't answered my email yet."

"I can't believe you thought blackmailing our

own grandmother would work," I countered. "Do you really think she'll tell us if she did something horrible to Ms. X?" I shuddered, still trying not to think about the skull-room vision.

"She'd better." Cass stood up, heading to the closet to grab shoes. "Because I was serious about telling Mom. I mean, we have no choice."

Just then there were twin pings from Cassie's phone and laptop. "Email alert," I said. "Maybe that's her now."

Cassie was already at her desk hitting keys on her laptop. I got up and looked over her shoulder. "I'm not sure who it's from. There's a video message."

"Don't click on that!" I yelped. "It could be a virus or something!"

Too late. Cassie had already clicked to open it. Typical. She never thinks things through until it's too late. Like trying to blackmail our possibly scary grandmother, for instance . . .

I forgot about that and gasped as a familiar face popped up on the video. "Ms. Xavier!" I cried.

Cass looked surprised. "Wait, I need to turn up the volume."

She cranked it up and started the video again. Ms. Xavier began the video reaching forward as if to adjust the camera, smiling and looking as happy as could be.

"Hello, twins!" she said cheerfully. "I heard you were worried about me, and I'm so sorry I won't be there to help you with your social studies project after all. I want you to know, that was the only thing that made me hesitate even briefly before accepting this amazing opportunity."

"Opportunity?" Cassie murmured.

I shushed her. My eyes widened as the camera panned out, showing more of the background. Ms. Xavier was in the skull room from my vision!

"But I just couldn't turn it down in the end," she went on, waving a hand at the creepy room. It was better lit than in my vision, but that wasn't such a good thing. It just meant we had an even better view of the skulls and other stuff—old books, weird-looking cloth dolls, drippy candles, dusty bottles full of dried insects, and more.

"Is that her apartment?" Cassie joked weakly.

I shook my head, listening as Ms. Xavier went on. "It's the biggest and best-funded study of the history and science of voodoo ever known," she exclaimed. "I don't know who recommended me for it, but I'm eternally grateful. It's already showing great potential for interesting discoveries. But unfortunately it means I've had to take a sabbatical from AMS for at least the rest of the year, maybe longer." She smiled sunnily. "I hope you'll let me know how your project turns out! Ta ta, twins!"

The video ended. I sat back, stunned.

"Wow," Cassie said, clicking off the email. "Crazy."

"Yeah. I guess this means Grandmother Lockwood didn't have her kidnapped after all."

"Not against her will, anyway." Cassie shook her head. "But you can't tell me she wasn't behind this sudden voodoo 'opportunity.' I mean, who else would ask Ms. X to do something like that? And who else would tell her we were worried about her so she'd make this video—the day after I sent that email?"

"I guess it had to be Grandmother Lockwood," I agreed. "I still feel guilty for suspecting her of all kinds of terrible stuff, though."

Cass shrugged. "Maybe we were a tad harsh on her, but she was definitely pretty sneaky," she pointed out. "And this proves she got my email. So why hasn't she answered it?"

"I don't know." I was only half listening as my brain worked out what all this meant. "But I guess I'm still mostly seeing good stuff after all."

"Oh. Right." She frowned. "Ms. X was probably thrilled about whatever that guy in the cape was doing in your vision."

"I just remembered something else," I said slowly. "Ms. Xavier was in that vision I had about Emily, remember? The one with the ribbon on her chair?"

"Oh yeah." Cassie nodded. "Weird. But you had that one before Ms. X left for Voodoo University, right? Maybe that meant there was still a chance she wouldn't go. Like, showing a possible future, not a definite one."

"But actually she did go, and the thing with Emily didn't happen, so the whole vision was bogus." I sighed. "Talk about confusing!"

"We already know none of the visions are sure things, right? Otherwise we couldn't change what we see." Cassie checked her watch. "We can figure all that out later. Right now, hurry and finish getting ready. I don't want to miss kickoff."

"You mean you don't want to miss getting a seat behind the home team bench so you can flirt with your trip buddy Brayden during the game?" I teased.

"Shut up." She rolled her eyes. "I never should've told you about that."

She'd filled me in on Brayden's "dare" on our way home from school yesterday. How adorable was that? I was super happy for my sister—especially since Brayden seemed like such a great guy. "It's not like I wouldn't have noticed when we all got on the bus next week," I pointed out, wandering over to the dresser to do my hair.

"Whatever. Are you worried about who the school's going to stick you with? What if you end up trip buddies with, like, Gabe Campbell or someone gross like that?"

I still didn't have a partner for the class trip. That

meant the school would assign me someone. Not ideal, but I was trying not to worry about it.

"Maybe I'll end up meeting someone nice," I said.

"Okay, Suzie Sunshine." She sounded skeptical. "But if you end up with Gabe, don't expect to hang out with me and Brayden."

Her computer pinged again. Cassie's eyes widened when she looked.

"It's from her!" she said.

I didn't need to ask who she meant. Dropping the hair elastic I'd just picked up, I rushed over.

The email from Grandmother Lockwood was short and not so sweet.

I received your message, and I trust you've heard from your teacher by now. Please refrain from threatening me in future, it's not at all useful. Also, your mother mentioned that your class is going to San Antonio next week. I'm afraid this could be dangerous for you two. Please be certain to cancel as soon as possible. I'll explain when I see you.

Love,

Your grandmother

Cassie was horrified. "She doesn't want us to go on the class trip? Why?"

"Dangerous? What do you think she means by that?" Feeling a little nervous, I grabbed my sister's hand.

The vision came immediately. I wasn't wearing the talisman, but I still had no trouble seeing the brighter Cassie that replaced the real one in front of me. Vision Cassie's eyes were wide as she watched Grandmother Lockwood embrace a man in the middle of a hilly street. And when the man pulled away, I recognized him—it was the shabby guy from our earlier vision!

Before I could get a good look at the background, Cassie yanked her hand away. "What?" she demanded.

I blinked at her, overwhelmed by what I'd just seen—and what it could mean. "Didn't you see it?" I asked.

She shook her head. "No visions here," she said. "But I can tell you had one. So spill. Was it about me and Brayden?"

"N-no." I tried to gather my thoughts, but they

were whirling around in my head like leaves in a storm. "You were there, but the vision was mostly about our grandmother. And I think . . ."

My voice trailed off. I was half afraid to say what came next.

"What?" Cassie demanded, giving me a sharp poke in the arm.

I took a deep breath, meeting her eye. "I think our father might still be alive!"

Turn the page for a sneak peek at what these
psychic sisters are up to in book four,
Double Cross!

CAITLYN

"MAYBE WE SHOULD text Grandmother Lockwood again," I said. "She might text us back if we tell her what I saw in my last vision."

My twin sister, Cassie, shot a cautious look toward the kitchen. Our mother was in there puttering around with something on the stove, humming under her breath. "We can talk about it later," Cass murmured, miming a lip-zip.

I sighed and leaned back on the sofa. It was Monday afternoon. Cass and I had come home from school about half an hour earlier, and Mom was supposed to leave for work right after dinner. It made sense to wait.

Cassie shot another look toward Mom, who was paying no attention to us. Then she mimed unzipping her lips.

"Anyway, we shouldn't be in such a hurry for Granny L to come back," she said quietly, grabbing the remote and turning up the volume on the goofy celebrity gossip show she was watching. "She might convince Mom not to let us go on the class trip."

I picked at my cuticles, thinking about that. The sixth-grade class trip to San Antonio was just three days away. It would be the first time Cassie and I had been back to our old hometown since Mom had landed a job on the police force in tiny Aura, Texas.

But a lot had happened in that couple of months. For one thing, Cassie and I had actually become friends again. Everyone said we looked exactly alike, from our big brown eyes to our skinny legs. But the thing was, we were very different in all kinds of other ways. That had made us drift apart for a while.

Then, shortly after the move, we'd discovered something weird. As in, *really* weird. We were both having crazy visions!

It happened when we touched someone. Oh, not every time—thank goodness for that! But we never knew when it might happen. All we had to do was brush up against someone, and we might suddenly find ourselves right smack in the middle of a vision about that person.

A vision of the future.

I know that sounds totally wackadoodle. But it was true! Grandmother Lockwood had confirmed it. She was our dad's mom, and we hadn't known she existed until she sent us a package with some family heirlooms in it for our twelfth birthday—and then showed up on our doorstep herself! She'd explained that Cass and I had inherited something called the Sight. It ran in the Lockwood family—our dad had had it, too.

Speaking of our dad, Mom had always told us he'd died when we were too young to remember. We'd had no reason to doubt that story until recently. Then I'd had another vision. It had showed our grandmother standing on a hilly street, embracing a man who looked an awful lot like the one and only picture we'd ever seen of our dad.

Needless to say, I really, really wanted to talk to Grandmother Lockwood about that vision. But she'd left town without telling us where she was going or when she'd be back. The only thing she had told us was not to go on the class trip. She didn't say why—just that it could be dangerous. Scary, right?

Not that I was thinking much about the trip right then. I stared at the TV, where some boy band was dancing around.

"I just wish . . . ," I began.

The shrill ring of the house phone interrupted me. Yes, Mom is still old-fashioned enough to have a landline. I leaned over and grabbed the cordless handset from the coffee table.

"Hello, Waters residence, Caitlyn speaking," I said.

"Cait?" The voice on the other end of the line sounded muffled but familiar. "Is your mother there?"

"Aunt Cheryl?" For a second I wasn't sure it was Mom's sister. She sounded weird—sort of tense. "Hi, funny you should call right now," I said. "Cass and I were just talking about San Antonio—you know, our class trip is—"

"Cait, I really need to talk to Deidre," Aunt Cheryl cut me off. "Is she there?"

"Um, sure, hang on." I raised my eyebrows at Cassie as I lowered the phone. "Hey Mom, Aunt Cheryl's on the phone!"

"Thanks." Mom bustled out of the kitchen and took the phone. "Cheryl? I don't have much time to talk, I have to . . ."

Her voice trailed off as she listened to whatever her sister was saying. Then she abruptly turned away and hurried toward her bedroom. A second later we heard the door click shut.

"That was weird." I stared toward the hallway leading to the bedrooms. "Aunt Cheryl sounded kind of—"

"Quiet!" Cassie ordered, suddenly leaning forward. She cranked up the volume on the TV another few notches.

I glanced at the picture. A reporter was talking, looking excited. Behind her was a headshot of a pretty young Asian woman with blue streaks in her hair.

"Is that Sakiko Star?" I asked.

Cassie shushed me again. I took that as a yes. Sakiko was Cassie's favorite singer these days. I liked her music just fine, but I wasn't that interested in celebrity gossip.

The story was about some escalating feud between Sakiko and her eccentric billionaire neighbor. The reporter looked super excited as she talked about how the guy was dumping his trash in the Dumpster that Sakiko had rented for a home renovation project.

". . . and while Mr. Jeffers denies everything," the reporter went on breathlessly, "the definite clues are parrot poop and a lot of empty sardine cans."

"Sardine cans?" I echoed with a laugh. "Really, that's a clue?"

"Uh-huh." Cassie's eyes were locked on the TV screen. "Apparently the neighbor guy always smells like fish."

I snorted. Then I blinked as a picture of two neighboring mansions popped up on the screen. One of them looked a bit shabby—a few windows were boarded up, and the yard and shrubs were all overgrown.

But I was focused on the other house. "Wait, why does that place look familiar?" I said slowly, trying to figure it out.

Cassie shrugged. "Duh. That's Sakiko's place. You've probably seen it on TV."

"Oh." The picture cut away to a video of Sakiko singing onstage. I still had a nagging little feeling that the house was familiar somehow. But I figured my sister was probably right—she was always watching stuff about Sakiko online and on TV. I'd probably seen the star's house a dozen times without really taking it in, and now it was lodged in my brain along with a zillion other useless bits of trivia.

Losing interest, I headed toward the bathroom. It was down the narrow hall that led off the living room to the rest of the house. Mom's bedroom came first, and as I passed, I could hear her on the phone even through the closed door. She sounded kind of upset.

That was even weirder than Aunt Cheryl's behavior on the phone. Deidre Waters wasn't the type of person who got upset by much. Otherwise, she wouldn't have survived her many years in the military, let alone the police academy. Sure, she yelled at Cassie and me sometimes, especially when Cass missed curfew or I forgot to put my dirty clothes in the hamper. But getting angry or annoyed or exasperated wasn't the same as getting *upset*.

I paused by the door, torn between guilt and curiosity. Aunt Cheryl called all the time—she and Mom were close. But today had seemed different. It was obvious she hadn't just called to chat and catch up, or she would have talked to me for a while before asking for Mom. And Mom wouldn't have locked herself in her room to talk to her.

So what was going on?

I couldn't resist leaning a little closer. The doors in our house were thin, but Mom's voice was pretty muffled. Still, I could hear a few words here and there—something about a keychain, and then "It can't be" and "He's dead, Cheryl. I made my peace with that years ago."

I gulped, flashing back again to that vision. What if it was true? What if my dad really was still alive? But how could Aunt Cheryl possibly know that, if Mom and Grandmother Lockwood had no idea?

Suddenly I realized that Mom's voice had stopped. I jumped away from the bedroom door and reached for the bathroom knob. A split second later, Mom burst out of her room.

She spotted me standing there. I guessed maybe I looked guilty, because her eyes narrowed.

"Um, hi," I said as cheerfully as I could manage. "How's Aunt Cheryl?"

"Fine." Mom's voice was almost a growl. She strode past me into the bathroom. The door slammed shut behind her, and the lock clicked.

Don't miss these books by
TIA & TAMERA MOWRY

HARPER
An Imprint of HarperCollinsPublishers

www.harpercollinschildrens.com